LAURA MILLER
NATIONAL BESTSELLING AUTHOR
of *Butterfly Weeds*

a bird
ON A
windowsill
a love story

This book is a work of fiction. Names, characters, businesses, places and incidents are the product of the author's imagination or are used fictitiously. Any resemblance to actual events, locals or persons, living or dead, is coincidental.

ISBN-13: 978-1523377008
ISBN-10: 1523377003

Printed in the United States of America.

Cover design by Laura Miller.
Cover photo, title page photo (girl) © Nadya Korobkova /Shutterstock.com.
Cover photo, second title page photo, *The End* page photo (watercolor) © pilipa/Fotolia.com.
Quote pages photo, chapter headings photo (birds) © beaubelle/Fotolia.com.
Dedication page photo, contents page photo, quote pages photo, chapter headings photo, acknowledgments page photo (feather) © molokot/Fotolia.com.
Author photo © Neville Miller.

To the One who rides upon the wings of the wind,
For second chances.

CONTENTS

People say birds are a bad omen. But I'm not so sure because while the only bird I ever knew tore my world in two, I loved every single moment of it.

To Madi,

A Bird *on a* Windowsill

LAURA MILLER

Hope you enjoy Salem &
Savannah!
So nice to meet you!

[signature]

Never regret something that once made you smile.

~Unknown

Prologue One
Salem

"Who do you choose, Vannah?"

My tone is even, an attempt to hide the uncertainty in my voice.

Her gaze immediately casts down to the floor. I watch as she squeezes her eyes shut, bites her bottom lip—a nervous habit of hers—and then slowly raises her head.

My heart beats out a rhythm in my chest. If I had to, I'd put it to some wild, sped-up version of *My Generation*. There's a lump in my throat. I try like hell to swallow it down, but it doesn't go anywhere. I'm terrified of what she's about to say, and yet, against all odds, I'm hopeful.

She looks up. Her eyes open. A green sea floods the little room in which we're standing. I close my eyes and try not to drown in her essence. In my mind, she's five years old. Her hair is short. She calls my name. She takes my hand. She's six, seven, eight, nine, ten, eleven years old. Her hair is long. She makes me laugh. She's beautiful. She's perfect. *Twelve, thirteen, fourteen, fifteen, sixteen. Seventeen.* I think I love you. I think I always have. *Eighteen, nineteen, twenty, twenty-one, twenty-two.* I miss you. I love you. I always will. *Twenty-three.* Choose me.

I open my eyes and look up just as her lips part. Her eyes are dark, holding in her secret. I try to read them, but I can't.

I take a breath.

And then there are words—soft words, delicately dripping from her full, red lips. I hear them, but to me, they're just the sound of a bird taking off from a windowsill.

People say birds are a bad omen. But I'm not so sure because while the only bird I ever knew tore my world in two, I loved every single moment of it.

My name is Salem Ebenezer—or Eben, if you're Savannah. Short *e*. Short *e*. And most of all, short for Ebenezer. And this is the story about me and Savannah Catesby. Savannah Elise Catesby, that is. Though, to me, she was always just *Vannah.*

I met Vannah when we were very young—just five years old. She had short, blond hair and soft green eyes.

Though, as we grew older, her hair got longer and her eyes, darker and more mysterious.

I loved Vannah. I loved her for her unruly laugh and the way she made me feel. To her, I wasn't the smallest and scrawniest boy in the first grade. To her, I was...me.

And I loved her because she would always pick me first for her kickball team. And I loved her for those times I forgot my lunch, and she shared hers with me. But most of all, I loved Vannah because she had this innate ability to make everyone around her feel loved.

But somewhere in the midst of junior high—in the midst of zits and a squeaky voice and an awkward way of getting around, both physically and in conversation, I changed—we changed. That was about the time I realized that I loved Vannah not only for the way she made me feel and the occasional ham and cheese sandwich, but also for our long talks under the stairs after school and the way her mouth moved when she laughed. And I fell in love with the way she ate peanut butter cups—from the inside out—and how she always knew when something was wrong...or new...or different.

And without me even realizing it, the hours turned into days, and the days, to years, and before either of us knew, I think, we were fifteen and in high school. And that was the first time, I think, that I noticed Vannah's long, tan legs....and the precarious way my name rolled off her tongue...and how she made just pulling her hair back or signing her name in those long, drawn-out curves, somehow sexy.

And it was then that I realized I loved her for those things, too.

But still, for whatever reason—I can't tell you—I

never told her that. I never told Vannah that I loved our long talks or her long legs. Not right away anyway. In fact, it wasn't until she had moved away and had come back for a summer, the year we both turned eighteen, that I finally got up the courage.

It was the summer of the Polaroid, and God must have taken pity on my oblivious self because he smiled down on me, and he gave me those three little words—and a second chance to tell her how I feel.

July 6, 2001. That was the day that I finally realized that I not only loved Vannah for everything she was, but I, plain and simple, loved Vannah.

And I told her that. I told her that—that same day I realized it. On a soft night in the middle of Hogan's slab, I told Savannah Catesby that I loved her. And I only remember the date because she said it back.

I'm twenty-three now. It's July 12, 2007. I'm still in love with that little girl with the unruly laugh and the long, wild hair and the dark stare and the tireless heart. And I know she still loves me.

But now, she's standing at the door, her dark green eyes slicing open the distance between her gaze and mine. And I'm just staring back at her. And three thoughts are all that are on my mind:

I love this girl.
I love this girl.
I love this girl.

She takes a breath. I hold mine. And with that, a silent thought slips into my cadence.

I love this girl.
I love this girl.
I love this girl.
Choose me.

Choose me.

Prologue Two

Savannah

I've come to learn two truths about love.

One: The fall is the easy part.
Two: It's best not to fall.

My name is Savannah Catesby. And this is a love story. It's not pretty. It's not poetry. It doesn't even have a happy ending. But I guess that's partially due to the fact that it's not over, yet. And honestly, I'm not sure it will ever really be over. I'm not sure *love*—of any kind— is a thing you *get over*. And it's definitely not a thing you get over when it comes to Salem Ebenezer— my oldest friend.

And really, in the end, I just wish we had more time. I wish we had a dozen lifetimes to get this right.

But of course, we don't.

We only have this one—and it's short.

Way too short.

I love Salem. I always have. But then, there's something else I've also learned about love: *Sometimes the hearts we steal are not the hearts we were ever meant to keep.*

Chapter One

Salem
(Five Years Old)

Day 1

"Who are you?"

My back stiffens. And for a second, I can't breathe.

"I can see you. You're not a ghost, are you?"

I slowly catch my breath and then shake my head.

"What's your name?"

"Salem." My voice cracks, and I work fast to clear my throat. "Salem Ebenezer."

She drops her gaze to the water in the little stream for a moment, and then just as quickly, her eyes are back on me.

"Ebenezer?"

I nod once.

"Do people call you Eben?"

I shake my head *no*.

"Then, I'll call you Eben."

I feel my face twist into a question mark. "Why?"

She shrugs her narrow shoulders and goes to poking a stick at some soft red clay. "I don't know."

It's quiet then. There's a sound of a truck—like a dump truck—off in the distance, but other than that, it's quiet.

I watch her. She slips off her tan sandals and dips her bare feet into the water. The water must be cold because she lifts her toes fast and goes back to poking at the red clay, instead. I watch as she stamps out a pile of little holes and then makes them disappear by pressing her palm hard to the clay.

I have been coming down here for almost a week now, spying on her. And I know I'm not supposed to be spying, but I can't help it. Every day about this time, she comes to this little stream that runs through the center of town, and she pokes at the mud or drops rocks into the water and watches them sink. And most times, I can't hear what she's saying, but I can see her lips moving, like she's making up stories as she goes. I like being a spy, and plus, she's fun to watch. But today, I just couldn't watch her anymore. Today, I decided I wanted to be in her stories. And that's when I stepped out from behind the trees.

She looks up at me, and my breath gets caught in my throat. I don't say anything as her stare hangs on me for what feels like one of Reverend Cantrell's whole sermons. And I feel like runnin', and I probably should, but I don't.

"What are you doing here anyway?"

I shrug. "I don't know."

I sure ain't gonna tell her I'm spying.

She narrows her eyes at me. "Well, how'd you get here?"

"I walked."

I watch as she pushes her lips to one side of her mouth—just like a grown-up does when they don't know whether they should laugh at you or scold you.

"Well, do you wanna play with me?"

When I don't say anything right away, she picks up a rock and throws it into the water. Her hair is cut short, kind of like my sister's. She looks nice. She's a girl, but I don't got much choice at this time of day. There usually ain't any kids around here until evening.

"Well?" she asks, a little impatient, this time.

I quickly drop my eyes to the dirt at my sneakers.

"I guess," I eventually say. And I follow that with a shrug.

"Well, come on."

She waves me over. And now, all of a sudden, instead of having the urge to run away, I have the urge to run to her. But I don't want her to think I like her, so I don't.

And the next thing I know, I'm sitting down on a rock next to her. I grab a stick, too. There are all kinds of sticks around. I look up. There's a maple tree hanging above us. They must have all come from it.

"I've never seen you here before," she says, jabbing her stick into the ground near my shoe. It's almost as if she's trying to get me to move my foot. I press it harder into the ground.

"What are you thinking about?" she asks.

My eyes quickly find hers.

"What? Me?"

She only nods.

"Trees and sticks...and you trying to poke my foot."

Her eyes light up, and her smile gets big. "How did you know?"

I shrug. "I just knew," I say, proudly.

"You're on my telescope."

"Your what?" I quickly pick up my foot and look at the ground under it. There's nothing there.

"This is the moon," she says, pointing at all the little holes she's poked into the ground. "And I'm looking at the stars through my telescope." She bounces a stick, as if it's walking, to the place my shoe just was. And then she jabs it hard into the ground.

I picture my foot still being there, and I let out a thankful breath that it's not.

"My friend, Dillon, says the moon's made out of cheese," I say.

She gives me a funny look and then just stares at me.

"What are those?"

I follow her eyes to my pocket.

"Gummy worms," I say, tugging on the little bag. "You want some?"

I hand her the bag, and she takes it and opens it with her little hands. And then her eyebrows squish together.

"Why are there gummy bears in here, too?"

She pulls out a worm with one hand and a bear with the other.

I shrug. "I just put them together, so I didn't have to carry two bags."

I watch as she holds the two gummies side by side, as if she's examining the two closely.

10

"Why have I never seen you before?" she asks, shoving both the bear and the worm into her mouth and biting down hard.

"I don't know," I say, squashing the urge to tell her that she probably hasn't seen me because I'm good at hiding. "I usually stay around the sawdust pile."

Her eyes are back on mine fast. So fast, it makes me jump.

"At the lumberyard?"

"Yeah," I say. "My dad owns it."

"Can we go there?"

I lift my shoulders and then let them fall. "Yeah, if you want."

She jumps up, stuffs the gummies into her pocket and rubs her hands together. Then she brushes off the back of her dress. "Let's go then."

And as quick as my dog can lick up my leftovers, she slips on her sandals and starts walking. I throw my stick down and follow her.

She's a fast walker, and I have to run a little to catch up.

"What's your name anyway?"

"Savannah," she says, without missing a beat.

I think about it for a second. "Does anyone call you Vannah?"

"No," she says, short and sweet.

"Well," I ask, timidly, "can I call you Vannah?"

"Why?"

I feel her eyes on me, but for some reason or another, I don't look up. I just keep my eyes on the dirt and the grass at our feet. "I don't know."

I don't hear anything for a while, so I lift my head and catch her smiling at me. And right then and there, I decide that her smile is nice.

"Okay," she says. "You can call me *Vannah.*"

I feel my grin getting bigger, as I shove my hands into my pockets.

"Why are you always at that stream?" I ask.

"How do you know I'm always there?"

I meet her eyes and notice they're green. But then I quickly look down.

"I mean, today," I say, instead. "Why were you there today?"

She shrugs. "My uncle works at the paper."

"Oh," I say. "Does he write all those stories?"

"Yeah."

"Well, then that makes sense."

"What makes sense?"

"Oh." My fingers nervously fidget in my pockets. "Nothing."

There's a puddle in our path. We both jump over it.

"Do you live around here?" she asks.

"Yeah, I live right outside of town. I'm gonna start school soon."

"Where?"

"Allandale Elementary."

"Me too," she says, giving me another nice smile.

I smile back, and then I concentrate on walking. We cut a path straight through Mr. Witte's yard and across Maupin and Elm streets. And then she sticks her hand into the pocket of her dress and pulls out something shiny.

"Here," she says, holding the shiny thing out to me.

"What is it?" I ask, taking it from her.

"It's a key. I found it, but you can have it."

I turn it over in my hand. "What's it to?"

She tilts her head back and squints her eyes up at the sky, most likely to keep the sun out. "Probably some big star tower...with a big, swirly staircase and a big hole in the ceiling where you can see the sky. And it's probably got a big telescope in it, too, so you can see the stars...up close."

I look at the key with wide eyes. "Really?"

"Probably." She shrugs.

"Well, then why are you giving it to me? Don't you want it?"

"Yeah, but you're better at finding things."

I hold the key out in front of me. A little ray of sunlight shines through the hole at the top and makes me shut my eyes

She's right, though. I am good at finding my grandpa's glasses when he loses them. But how does she know that?

"How do you know I'm better at finding things?"

She lifts one shoulder. "You found me."

I think about it and then nod. "I guess you're right."

"So," she says, "if you find that star tower, you come find me, and then we can spend all night looking up at the moon and dancing alongside the stars."

"Wait. It has stars...inside of it?"

"Yeah, they live on the walls?"

She says it like it's something I should have known. I nod, approvingly.

"You find it. You come find me. Okay?"

I look at her and then back at the key before squeezing it into my palm.

"Okay," I agree.

We walk a few more steps.

"Vannah?"

13

"Yeah?"

"Are you mine?"

She gives me a funny look—like she's just discovered I'm an alien or something.

"I mean," I say, feeling embarrassed. "Are you my friend?"

She smiles. "Yes."

I let go of a thankful breath.

"Eben?"

"Yeah?"

"Are you mine?" She's looking at me, grinning wide.

I nod. "Yep."

"**W**hat do you got there, boy?"

I look down at the little piece of metal in my hand. "A key," I say.

"Let me see it."

I hold it out in front of me, and Grandpa's old, wrinkly hand reaches for the key. I watch him as he goes to examinin' it. He lets his glasses slide down his nose as he turns it over and mouths under his breath the random letters written on the piece of metal.

"Hmm," he says. "Looks like a key to some toolbox, maybe."

"A toolbox?" I try not to sound disappointed.

"Yeah," he says, still looking at it. "Where'd you get this from?"

I shrug. "That girl that's been hangin' out at the paper gave it to me."

"Aah," he breathes out. "A gift from a girl."

"It wasn't a gift," I shoot back. "She just found it and said that I could have it."

"Aah, son," he breathes out again, pushin' his thick glasses back up the bridge of his nose. "When a girl gives you somethin', it's special."

I wrinkle my nose in disgust. Grandpa's talking crazy again. He does that sometimes. I go to fiddlin' with a string that's come lose on my shirt—just to pass the time. Mom says it ain't right to walk away when someone's talking—even when you don't want to hear what they're talking about.

"Girls are treasures, son." He points the key at me while eyeing me from over the top of his glasses. "And when one gives you somethin', it's like she's givin' you a piece of her treasure."

"That's crazy, Grandpa. Girls aren't treasure."

"Oh, sure they are."

I stick my tongue out and roll my eyes to the back of my head.

"Your grandma is."

I stop and think about it for a second and then shrug.

"Yeah, maybe Grandma," I admit. "But that's it."

"Well, your mother is, too," Grandpa offers.

I shrug again. "I guess so. But that's it."

"Your sister?"

"No way!" I say.

His deep, full laugh fills the air. "Son, all I'm sayin' is that if a girl gives you somethin', you hold onto it." He pauses and then points a crooked finger in my direction. "Better yet," he says, "you hold onto her."

I stick my tongue out, resisting the urge to roll my eyes back in my head again. Mom says if I do it too much, my eyes will stay there.

"You'll find that out the hard way sooner or later." He gives me his Grandpa look—the one that's somewhere in between his normal face and a smile. "We all do."

I push my mouth to one side and lazily shrug my shoulders before turning to find Grandma. She's always got some kind of chocolate to give me when I see her, and chocolate's a lot better than whatever Grandpa's tryin' to feed me right now.

"Son," Grandpa says, stopping me. "You forgot your treasure."

"Aah," I say, starin' at the little silver key in his wrinkly hand. "You can keep it, Grandpa. I thought it was to a star tower."

"A star tower?"

"Yeah," I say, sounding a little defeated. "It's a place where you can see the stars up close."

"Like an observatory?"

I shrug. "Maybe." I don't know what that is.

Grandpa just looks at me and then smiles and sets the key onto the edge of the table. "Okay, but I'm still just gonna leave it here for you, son."

I sigh and venture off to find Grandma, but I don't even get two steps into the hallway when I hear Grandpa's old, scratchy voice again.

"Son."

I stop, but I don't turn around.

"I've been known to be wrong...a time or two," he says. "That there might very well be a key to a star tower. ...A big one."

I still don't turn around, until after I hear the paper rustling behind me. Then slowly, I peek back around the corner. Grandpa's taken a seat in his big easy chair, and he's got the paper opened wide in front of his face.

I stare at him for a few seconds, and then carefully, I tiptoe back into the room, quietly grab the key and stuff it deep inside my pocket.

Chapter Two

Salem
(Eight Years Old)

Day 1,095

"**D**illon, go get that shovel. We can scoop it up with that."

I cup my hands and dig into the powdered wood chips. Dillon and I are trying to see if we can make the biggest sawdust mountain we've ever made.

"Dillon," I shout over my shoulder. "The shovel."

I don't hear him move, so I look up to see what he's doing.

He's staring off into the distance at something.

"What's she doing here?" he asks.

I stand up taller and squint my eyes to try and see what he's looking at. And as soon as I get a good look, I see Vannah, walking across the back field toward us.

I shrug. "I don't know." I go and grab the shovel myself and start scooping more sawdust onto our mountain. "Maybe she can help."

I glance back at him, and he gives me a funny, side-eyed look.

"But she's a girl."

I ignore Dillon, and a minute later, Vannah is facing the both of us.

"What are you guys doing?" she asks.

"Makin' a mountain," I say.

"Can I help?"

"Yeah," I say.

Vannah starts scooping the sawdust into her hands. And when her little hands can't hold anymore, she adds the sawdust to the top of the pile that Dillon and I have already started.

"You love her, don't you?"

Vannah and I both stop and turn toward Dillon.

"That's what it is," Dillon says. "You love her, don't you, Salem?"

He gives me a devilish smile, and I don't like it. But I just ignore him and go back to shoveling.

"You looove her," he sings, drawing out the *L* word.

I stop, quickly turn and face Dillon.

"I don't love her," I say to him.

"You do, too. You love Savannah Catesby."

I can feel my ears getting hot. "I don't love her," I say, louder this time.

"Yes, you do," he shouts.

I stand up straighter and throw the shovel hard to

the ground. "I don't either," I shout.

"You do, too," Dillon screams back.

He gets too close, and I shove him backwards.

"She's just a stupid girl," I say. "I don't even like her."

Both Dillon and Vannah are quiet, as my scream echoes between the two tin buildings, bouncing off the walls as if it's a dirty word.

I feel bad for what I just said. I look at Vannah. Her eyes are getting red.

"Vannah," I say, sheepishly.

Her lip starts to quiver, and then her mouth turns down into a frown. I try to think of what to do next, as a tear trickles down her cheek.

My eyes go to Dillon. I can tell he doesn't know what to do, either. He's on the ground now, staring at Vannah. He looks just as scared as I feel.

And just like that, Vannah takes off running. And I take off running after her.

"Vannah," I call to her. But it doesn't do any good. She doesn't stop running.

It takes me a minute, but I finally catch up to her.

"Vannah, I didn't mean it."

She stops and immediately turns away from me, covering her face.

"Go away."

I think about going away, but I don't want to leave her, so I stay.

"Vannah."

I touch her shoulder. And then I close my eyes and wait for her to slug me. But a few seconds go by, and she doesn't.

I slowly force my eyelids open, and she's facing me. Her eyes are puffy and red, and she's sniffling.

"You said I was a stupid girl."

"You're not a stupid girl," I say.

She keeps her red stare on me. I feel sad, too. I'm sorry for what I said. I'm sorry for making her cry.

"You're a smart girl," I say. "I'm a stupid boy."

My eyes slowly fall to the ground, and I dig my toe into the grass, until the tip of my shoe is covered in dirt.

"You said you didn't like me."

I shake my head back and forth. "I lied."

"So, you do like me?"

I look into her teary eyes, and I nod.

It feels as if two days go by, but eventually, her lips start to turn into a smile.

"Don't lie again," she demands.

"I won't," I promise.

And before I even realize what's happening, she wraps her arms around me. She hugs me, and it's the weirdest feeling in the world—to be hugged by her. My first instinct is to pull away and push her to the ground. That's what I should do. That's what Dillon would do. And if she were my sister, that's what I'd do. But for some reason or another, I don't. I just stand there, and I let her hug me. I let her hug me because I like her hug. I like the way it feels. But mostly, I like her hug because, out of all the girls I've ever met, this one's my favorite.

Chapter Three

Savannah
(Thirteen Years Old)

Day 2,920

"Three-pointer," I say.

I'm at Eben's. My mom and dad are at a parent-teacher conference for my sister. I had three choices: Stay at home and do homework, go with them or come over here. The first one was a definite *no*; the second sounded even more boring than the first. So, this was a no-brainer. Plus, Eben's mom was making chicken and dumplings tonight. And since I don't pass up his mom's chicken and dumplings, I left my house before dinner.

I shoot the little basketball at the goal stuck to

Eben's closet door. It hits the rim and bounces onto Eben.

"Nice shot, V," he says, catching the ball.

I narrow my eyes at him but still smile.

"Are you ever going to get new sheets?"

He looks at the bed covers surrounding me. I secretly like his Spiderman sheets, but I feel as if it's my duty to point out the fact that he *is* in junior high now and he *still* has sheets that look like comic books.

"Look who's talking."

"What?"

"Vannah, you've got purple cats all over your sheets."

"Cats are cool, though."

"Yeah, well, so is Spiderman."

We both look at each other. Neither of us wants to be the first to laugh.

It's usually him. But this time, it's me. I laugh first, and then, so does he.

I lie back on his bed and kick my feet up onto his sky-blue wall.

"Do you think we can see it yet?"

He shrugs. "Maybe."

A second later, he's crawling over me to get to the window.

"Watch it," I say. "Your pokey elbows are stabbing my ribs."

He stops and hovers over me. "My elbows aren't pokey."

I notice his eyes on mine, and I stop and look at them. I've always taken notice of Eben's eyes. His eyes are the first thing everyone notices when they see him. They're this perfect shade of light—almost the color of that sawdust at his dad's lumberyard—against his almond skin.

But tonight, I don't just notice his eyes; I feel them. I feel him looking at me—as if he's not just looking at me, but he's looking into me. It makes me feel exposed somehow. It makes me feel as if he's just discovered a secret of mine. And a part of me wonders if he has.

But it's only a moment. And then it's gone. And then his eyes drop, and he pushes off of the mattress and goes to the window.

I can't move. For a few seconds, I just lie there, staring at the white ceiling, wondering what secret he took with him.

"I think it's dark enough."

His voice forces my attention to him. He's standing in the window, still looking out of it. I sit up and watch him.

He's not the tallest boy in our class. In fact, he's just my height. But his feet and hands are big, like he's got more growing to do. And his hair is a little longer than most boys I know, even with its curls.

I smile to myself and watch him stare out that big window. I don't think of other boys like I think of Eben. Other boys are just boys. But Eben is *Eben*.

"We should go and look," he says, turning back toward me.

I jump a little and then quickly clear my throat.

"Yeah," I say. "We should."

He looks at me as if he just missed something, which he did. He missed the part where a little thought crossed my mind—a little thought that said I just *might* have a crush on Salem Ebenezer.

I stand and smooth out my hair with my fingers, trying to hide my thoughts. "Well, let's go," I say.

He's wearing a smile, but he gives me a funny look.

I just ignore it, as I turn and silently trudge out of his bedroom and to his back door.

It's dark outside when I push through the door. And until my eyes adjust, it's hard to see. But I keep walking. I know the path to his trampoline by heart. And soon, I reach the metal steps and easily crawl up them.

The black canvas is cool against my skin. I lay my back against the stretched surface. And seconds later, Eben's lying down right beside me.

"There it is," I say, pointing at the night sky.

His eyes follow my finger.

"Yep," he says, "there it is."

Hale-Bopp. It looks like a really big star with a long, glowing tail. The news says it's one of the brightest comets anyone alive has ever seen. It got here in January, and it's been here ever since. Eben and I spend every night we get just looking up at it because it won't be here long—that's what the news says, anyway. Although, I do hope they're wrong.

"I hope it stays here forever," I whisper.

"Maybe it will," he says, never taking his eyes off the sky.

"I could look at it forever."

He doesn't say anything. And for a long time, we just stare off into the black.

"Eben?" I ask, breaking the silence.

"Yeah?"

"Will you always look up at the sky with me—like even when Hale-Bopp's gone?"

He tilts his face my way and meets my stare.

"Yeah," he says. A little smile plays on his face.

"Even when we're old—even when we're like twenty or thirty?"

He nods. "Even when we're forty."

I smile, feeling content.

"Vannah?"

I turn my face his way.

"Why do you like the sky so much?"

I return my attention to Hale-Bopp, as my mind flashes back to my childhood.

"Ever since I met you, you've been looking up at that sky," he says.

I lift my shoulders a little.

"My grandma always said the sky feeds the soul," I say. "She said, every once in a while, you just have to look up." I shift my face back in his direction. "When I was little, after my grandpa had passed away, my grandma and my sister and I would go out into the backyard at night and lie in the grass and count the stars. My grandpa was my grandma's world. And I think after he passed, the moon and the stars became my grandma's world. We looked up at that sky so much that I guess it just kind of became mine, too. It was like my second home."

He nods, as if satisfied. And then, slowly, our gazes return to that big comet living up there in my home away from home.

Chapter Four

Salem
(Fourteen Years Old)

Day 3,285

"Vannah, you have two choices."

"Just two?"

"Yes, just two."

She leans back against her beanbag and kicks up her feet onto the belly of a stair. Every day at three o'clock, we meet under the stairs in the school's new addition. No one ever comes back here. In fact, I'm convinced people got so used to not having the extra space that they plumb forgot it was even here altogether.

But anyway, me and Vannah meet here every day at the same time—have been for almost a year now.

"Okay, what are they?" she asks.

I smile because I like that she likes to play my games.

"Okay, you could live your entire life in the middle of nowhere, completely alone—no family and no friends or..." I pause to think up the next part. I never really think any of this through. "Or," I start again, "you could live in just one, little room with ten other people for the rest of your life."

I finish, and I look over at her. She's staring at her white and gray Nikes and pulling on her bright pink shoe laces.

"Can I leave the room?"

"No," I say.

She settles more into her beanbag. About six months ago, she showed up here with that ugly, meatloaf-colored bag of beans. And when I looked at her, wondering where she had gotten it, she only shrugged and said Mr. Comb-over had enough and wouldn't miss it. I shrugged then, too. She was probably right. And either way, I knew that beanbag was staying here. And lucky for us, no one from Mr. Comb-over's office has ever said a word about it.

"Do I have to live in a room in the first one?" she asks.

I bite the inside of my cheek and think for a second. "No, you can go anywhere in the world. There's just no one in the world, I guess."

"And in the second one, I have to live in the same room...forever?"

"Yep," I confirm. "Forever."

"The whole world with no one or one room with

ten people...forever?" she asks.

"Right."

"Easy," she says. "The first one."

"But you won't have anyone to talk to."

She shrugs her shoulders, still playing with her shoe laces, endlessly tying big, pink double knots. "I think I'd rather be free to go anywhere I want than be confined to one, little room for the rest of my life."

"But who will you talk to?"

She cocks her head in my direction and smiles. "The birds."

I give her a disbelieving look. "You'll go crazy talking to birds."

"Or maybe I'll turn into one," she says, letting her foot dramatically fall from the stair and land on the floor with a thud.

She's looking at me with a scrunched-up nose and a silly, sideways smile. Her smile is distracting me so much that I forget what we're even talking about.

"Or maybe you could turn into a bird and sing to me," she says.

I smile, too, and instantly drop my gaze. It's a funny thought, but I like it all the same.

And when I look up again, our eyes lock.

This has happened once before—when we were in my room, on my bed, about a year ago. I didn't know what to do then. And I still don't know what to do now.

She keeps her eyes in mine. I can feel my heart start to race. I'm not sure what's going on, but I'm pretty sure I don't hate it. And soon, I feel my chest rise and fall, as every breath starts becoming necessary all of a sudden—as if someone just took away one of my lungs.

There's something about her eyes, something about her look. It makes me excited, nervous, uncomfortable—but a good uncomfortable.

I panic—just like I did the first time, and I drop my gaze first.

And after a moment, I notice her leaning back into her beanbag.

"Do you think they ever wonder where we go?"

I suck in a bunch of air and then force it all back out.

"What?" I ask, secretly trying to catch my breath.

She laughs easily. She could always laugh easily, no matter what firestorm was brewing around her. Laughing to Vannah was like breathing.

"Every day we disappear for the first fifteen minutes, and no one ever questions it," she says.

I shrug. We're supposed to be at Science Olympiad. It's an after-school program where you make things like paper airplanes and noodle bridges. And at the end of the year, all these schools get together and judge who made the best paper plane or who glued together the strongest noodle bridge. It sounds kind of nerdy, and it probably is, but there isn't much else to do out here in Wyandot County. So, Vannah builds airplanes, and I build bridges.

"What time is it?" she asks, interrupting my thoughts.

I hesitate for a second before I look at my watch.

"It's 3:15."

"You think we should surface?"

"I don't know. Maybe."

She stands up, and then I watch her kick the beanbag a couple times until it's propped up against the wall and out of sight to any passers-by.

"See you tomorrow?" she asks.

"Same place. Same time," I echo, out of habit.

She makes her way out from underneath the stairs, staying partially bent until she gets to the end and can stand up straight again.

"Vannah," I say, stopping her.

She turns and faces me. "Yeah?"

"Can I ask you something?"

"Yeah."

I don't say anything at first, and quickly, the silent moments turn awkward.

"What's wrong with you?" she asks.

Her eyes go to examining me right away, but she doesn't look worried. She looks more amused than anything.

"I, um," I stutter.

I feel my courage evaporating, as she narrows her eyes at me.

"Don't look at me like that."

"Like what?"

"Like I'm that little, scared, stupid boy that wandered up to you that first day."

Her face softens, and she laughs.

"I'm glad that you wandered up to me that day."

Her laughter melts into the concrete walls, making the air feel comfortable again.

I smile and fiddle with the pencil I always keep behind my ear.

"You were my first best friend," she says.

My smile grows a little wider.

"We'll always be best friends, right?" she asks.

Slowly, my grin starts to fade. I was kind of hoping she'd say we're something more than friends.

"Yeah," I mumble.

"Now, what were you going to ask me?"

"Oh," I say, averting my eyes. "Uh, I was wondering if...if you thought we were going to get a snow day tomorrow."

Vannah looks lost, almost as if she knew what I was going to say, and it wasn't that.

She crosses her arms and looks down at her tennis shoes. "Maybe," she says. "Maybe it'll snow enough."

It's quiet—so quiet, you can hear the voices of kids on the playground outside.

"Eben, is that what you were going to ask me?"

Her question sounds almost sad. I look up, and it happens again—just a moment too long, her eyes in mine.

I shrug. "I was just wondering," I say, awkwardly examining the gray linoleum tiles at my feet.

"Okay," she whispers.

I look up. And she keeps her stare on me for a little while longer, and then she smiles at me—just like she does every day, but today, her smile is smaller.

Nevertheless, I smile back—just like I do every day, even though, this time, it's forced.

And then, she's gone.

I wait a couple seconds, and then I fill up my lungs with as much air as I can fit into them, and then slowly, I let it all out and feel my head fall back against the wall.

Seconds disappear like raindrops into a pond. I close my eyes. A sigh follows.

"I like you, Savannah Catesby," I whisper. "I've always liked you."

But when I open my eyes again, there's only a gray, brick wall staring back at me.

Chapter Five

Salem
(Fifteen Years Old)

Day 3,650

"You have two choices."

She spins around in the padded office chair and faces me.

Strands of her hair come to rest on her chest. Her hair is long now—longer than it's ever been. And she's wearing make-up—the kind that makes her eyelashes longer and her eyelids black around their edges. But her eyes haven't changed. They're still the same shade of green they've always been.

"You can either eat pizza for every meal for the

rest of your life or you can eat whatever you want and only drink water for the rest of your life."

She looks out the window. "Hmm," she hums, "pizza or water."

The black and white clock on the wall ticks out a few slow seconds.

"Only water?" she asks, settling her gaze back on me.

I nod. "Only water."

"Pizza then," she says, right before she swivels back around and faces the computer screen again.

"Why?" I ask—because her answers have never been more important than her *whys*.

"My grandma's sweet tea."

That's all she says before moving a three of hearts to the two of hearts.

"How much more time?" she asks.

I look up at the clock. "One minute."

She lets out a puff of air. "Okay, I can beat this game."

I smile at her determination, even in something as small as a game of solitaire.

In one minute, our time will be over for the day. It used to be that our time was just beginning when that last bell rang. Now, though, since we started high school, it seems as if I only have these few stolen moments with her.

I grab my backpack and sling it over one shoulder just as Vannah puts her last king onto one of the decks and the cards begin cascading down the screen.

"See, told ya," she says, spinning around.

She's got a big smile on her face.

"You are quite the gamer."

She laughs and reaches for her bag, just as the bell

echoes its shrill siren out in the hallway.

"See you Wednesday, Eben."

"Same time, same place," I say, watching her as she makes her way out of the room.

She'll head to the gym, just like she does every day at three o'clock now. She plays volleyball on the school's varsity team. She's tall and strong, which makes for a pretty good athlete. *Me?* I'm not that tall, and I'm not that strong, and I'm definitely not much of an athlete, yet. My dad says he grew five inches in high school. I kept that in the back of my mind when I signed up for basketball this year. I want to be a basketball star, just like my dad. He holds the third-best scoring record here at this very high school.

But just in case I never hit that growth spurt, I have a backup plan. I play the drums in the school's band. I like to think that I'm a cool drum player because I have the beginnings of a garage band. Well, it's really just me; Dillon, who can sort of play the guitar; and Josh, who can only play one scale on the bass—so I'm not really sure that counts—but we call it a band, nonetheless.

But anyway, just like every day, Vannah looks back right before she escapes into the hallway, and she gives me her smile that I've come to expect.

I smile back, and then just like every day, I follow after her. But I don't get three steps into the hall when I look up and see her. And instantly, I realize that today isn't going to be *just* like every day.

She's stopped at the gym doors, and she's talking to a guy.

Is that Rylan Tennessee?

I watch them. She tilts her head back—almost as if she's laughing at something he said. Then she tucks her hair behind her ear. *Vannah doesn't do that.* I keep watching her. She touches his arm.

What is she doing? And what in the hell is Rylan Tennessee doing?

He's so close to her face.

Is he whispering something in her ear?

I stop right there in the middle of the hallway. And right there, my blood starts to boil. I never knew what that expression meant. I never could make hide nor hair out of it...until now.

People walk by me. Some brush up against me. Others just stop and stare at me. But I don't care because I'm watching someone else get way too close to Savannah Catesby.

My Savannah Catesby.

My Vannah.

Chapter Six

Salem
(Fifteen Years Old)

Day 3,650

I let every bit of air escape my lungs, and I beg my heart to slow down for a damn minute. And once it does that, I beg my legs to move again. And way too fast, I'm standing right in front of Savannah and Rylan Tennessee, as they stare blankly back at me.

"Vannah, can I talk to you?" I don't even acknowledge Rylan.

She looks at me with a question written on her face.

"Okay."

I watch as she turns her attention back to Rylan. "I'll call you after practice," she says to him. And then she smiles. *She smiles. At him.*

"Okay, babe, talk to you later," he says.

Babe? Babe? Who says that? He's either forty or he thinks he's Freddie Prinze Jr.

He glances at me before he turns to leave. We're eye to eye for only a split-second, but I know exactly what he said—because I said the same thing.

I watch him walk away from us. He's got this cool-guy swagger that I wish I had sometimes. And he's a giant—tall, with the beginnings of some muscles. And if that's not enough, he's a sophomore, and he's also a two-sport athlete. But up until just now—this very moment—I never thought about Rylan Tennessee. In fact, I don't think I had any opinion of the guy....or even one thought about him...ever. But now... Now, of course, that's all changed. Now, I despise him and his stupid cool-guy swagger.

"What did you want to talk about?"

I hear her voice, and it easily tears my stare away from model boy.

"What? That? Was what?" I stutter.

I don't think about the words before they spill out. They literally just spew out of my mouth, in no particular order.

She laughs, and her laugh seems to bring me back down to earth somehow. "What are you trying to say?"

"I just...," I start again. "Are you like, a thing or something with Rylan Tennessee?"

She looks at me, almost accusingly. "Rylan and me?"

Damn. Hearing his name roll off her lips just like it's her *own* name is like pumping poison straight into my blood. I just want to stop it before it ends up killing me.

I don't even wait for the answer I already know. After all, I just witnessed it.

"Since when?" I ask, impatiently.

"Since last weekend," she says. She adjusts her weight to her other leg and bows her head. I know she's trying to hide her smile.

I try not to puke in my mouth.

"Okay," I say, in total disbelief. I can feel my eyes burning. I squeeze them shut until I can't feel the burning anymore. "Okay," I say again, and then I leave her there. I don't say another word. I just turn and walk away.

"Eben."

I stop.

"Is that what you wanted to talk to me about?"

My eyelids instinctively fall over my eyes, and slowly, I find myself turning back toward her.

"I, uh..."

I stop. And my eyes catch on hers.

"I just wanted you to know that I'm still looking for your star tower."

A soft, guarded smile takes over her face. "Oh, really?"

"Yeah. I think I might be close."

Her warm eyes focus on mine for just a moment, and I get lost in them—for just a moment—until I just can't bear it anymore. And then I turn away.

"Eben."

I stop, but this time, I don't turn around.

"Is everything okay?"

"It's fine." I sigh to myself. "It's fine."

It's funny how a picture of a moment can just be frozen in your mind. For the next few days, I had that picture of her and "the one we won't speak of" plastered in my head, running on some kind of spinning wheel. Over and over again, it was just her and him. *Her and him laughing. Her and him getting too close. Her and him whispering stupid stuff into each other's ears. Over and over again.*

But the days came, and the days left, and eventually that picture turned over in my mind less and less. It still hurt the same, but it was easier to manage, I guess. If she was happy, I'd have to be happy for her...or at least, act like I was. After all, I was still her best friend, and according to her, that wasn't going to change. And for that, I loved her, and at the same time, hated life. But that's what you do when you love someone, right? You let them go?

Shit.

That advice is nothing but horse shit. *Who came up with that?*

When you really love someone, you don't let them go—mostly, because you can't. Nature won't allow it. But also, because you just don't. If I learned anything from my grandpa, I learned that you don't give up on people—especially girls. Now, you might put your life on hold, wait for cool-guy-swagger-model boy to screw up—which he will, eventually—and for her to come back to you. But you don't let her go. If you love her, you don't let her go.

Chapter Seven

Salem
(Sixteen Years Old)

Day 4,015

"Hi, Eben."

I look up, and Savannah is sitting across from me. She looks kind of sad.

"What's wrong? Did he do something?"

I sit up straighter and clench my fists, just as her sad look turns questioning.

"No." She shakes her head. "No."

"Then what is it?"

She grabs the extra carton of chocolate milk from my tray, and I watch as she tries to open it. *Every time.*

Every time she touches a little milk carton, she can't help but tear it to pieces trying to get into it. I usually watch until she starts getting really frustrated; it's kind of fun.

"Here," I say, taking the carton from her hands.

I easily open it from the side she didn't mangle. And then I set it back down in front of her.

"My dad got a job in South Carolina."

"South Carolina...?"

"Mount Pleasant. It's by Charleston."

I feel my eyebrows start to come together.

"Is he going to take it?"

She nods.

"So, your dad is going to live in South Carolina? That's going to be weird—not having your dad around."

I take a bite of my square fish sandwich.

"Eben, we're going with him."

"What?" I stop chewing.

"We're moving next month."

"Wait," I say, trying to swallow. "You're moving to South Carolina?"

She nods again.

"But that's like, on the east coast."

"Mm hmm," she says.

"That's halfway across the country."

"Mm hmm," she somberly hums.

"But we just started school."

"I know," she says.

I put down the sandwich and feel my eyes moving to the cafeteria's big glass doors. A girl is walking down from the parking lot. I mindlessly follow her path. I'm thinking of Vannah *not* being here. I'm thinking she can't *not* be here.

"Next month?" I ask, returning my full attention to her.

She nods, and I just stare at her. I'm not even completely sure what look is on my face. I know my mouth is cocked open, but I'm in so much shock I don't even care to fix it.

"That's fast," I say.

"I know."

I push my tray to the side. Suddenly, I'm not that hungry. Dillon and Josh set their trays down next to mine. But at their first sight of my face, they scoot to the other end of the table, instead.

"Does lover boy know?" I ask Vannah, ignoring Dillon and Josh.

"Yeah," she says, lowering her head.

"Oh course," I say. *Of course, he knew first.*

"I broke up with him."

"What?" The word comes out louder than I think either of us expected it to. Dillon and Josh both look up but then quickly go back to their square sandwiches after I shake them off.

"I'm sorry," I say to her. "But what did you say again?"

"I...just wanted a clean slate, I think. Rylan was nice...but... He's just not for me, I guess."

My chest is heavy, but from somewhere, I feel a smile rising up. Though, I quickly check it before it gets to my mouth, and I clear my throat, instead.

"I'm sorry," I say, rubbing the back of my neck.

"It's okay. It would have happened eventually."

I find her eyes, and I just can't help but grin a little after hearing that.

I knew it was going to happen sooner or later, but it's nice to hear she knew it, too.

43

"Don't," she says, starting to smile. "Don't you dare, Eben."

She lifts the carton of chocolate milk to her lips and takes a drink.

"What?" I ask.

"Come on. I know you didn't like Rylan."

"No," I say, dropping my gaze to the table. "I had nothin' against Rylan, really."

I glance back up at her and catch her stare. She's got this pout glued to her face—the look she gets when she knows I'm lying.

I shake my head. "It was *you* and Rylan I had a problem with."

"Eben!" She starts to laugh.

"What? You already knew that. Don't act so surprised."

She levels her eyes on me and holds them there for a few faultless moments. And it's in those moments that I see her. I see the girl I spent my whole childhood falling in love with. She's still there.

"Eben, I want to spend my last month here with you."

I cock my head to the side. I swear I'm hearing things.

"You wanna what?"

She shrugs. "I feel like we haven't spent more than ten minutes together in the last year."

"Well, that's true."

"Well, let's fix that," she says. "You're my best friend, and I'm leaving here soon. Let's have the most fun we've ever had."

I'm not sure exactly if I can believe what I'm hearing. Sure, *best friend* isn't maybe the best of titles, but if it gets me the opportunity to spend more time with her, I'll gladly take it. I'll gladly take whatever time I have left with her. I can't even think about her leaving. And I won't. I won't even entertain the thought, until I have to. Until then, it's me and her—*just me and her*. And I'm more than okay with just thinking about that.

"The most fun we've ever had, huh?"

I try to control my wild thoughts.

She nods her head and smiles.

"Okay," I say. "I think we can arrange that."

Chapter Eight

Salem
(Sixteen Years Old)

Day 4,022

"Salem."

My sister screams my name, and her high-pitched voice rattles the dishes in my mom's china cabinet.

"I'm right here. Geez. Lower it an octave, would ya?"

She gives me a mocking look and wiggles the receiver at me.

"It's Savannah," she says, chomping on her gum. "Don't talk too long. My boyfriend's supposed to call."

I take the receiver. "You have a boyfriend?"

I wait for an answer, but she just rolls her eyes and stalks off into the next room.

"Hey," I say, into the phone.

"Hey. It's Carter."

"What?"

"Her boyfriend is Carter."

"Carter Sutton?"

"Yeah."

"How did you know that?"

"They went to Winter Ball together."

"That makes you boyfriend and girlfriend?"

Savannah laughs into the phone. "Yeah, in junior high, it does."

I shake my head, still trying to wrap my brain around Shelby having a boyfriend. *She's only fourteen.*

"What are you doing?" Savannah asks, forcing me out of my thought.

"Oh, me? Nothing."

"Can I come over?"

"Uh, yeah." I rub the back of my neck. "Dillon and Josh are coming over to do some band stuff. But yeah, you can come, too."

"Good. I'll be there in ten minutes."

She hangs up the phone right away, but it takes me a few seconds. I can't stop thinking about how good it feels to have her come over. It's been a while, and I don't think I even realized how much I missed her, until now.

I hang up the receiver and stare at the phone's twisted, spiral cord.

"Just like old times," I say, smiling under my breath. "Just like old times."

"When you first told me you started a band, I might have pictured one with a clarinet and a tuba."

"No, you didn't."

She scrunches up her nose. "I did."

I sigh through my smile and take a seat next to her on a turned-over bucket.

"This is a huge step up," she adds.

"From a clarinet band? Really?"

Vannah laughs and nudges my ribs. It feels good— her next to me at my house again.

"But you really are good at it—playing the drums. I mean, who would have thought? You used to be so little and so awkward."

I laugh and turn my focus to the garage floor. "I was."

She's quiet, so I lift my head and meet her pretty stare.

"But you're not so little, and you're not so awkward anymore."

"No," I agree, "not as much."

I feel my cheeks grow hot, as she nudges my side with her elbow again. I'm glad the guys are long gone and can't see me blush.

"I remember when I was taller than you."

I nod. "I remember that, too."

Her smile is like a summer storm—something in between calm and dangerous.

"You didn't have to come watch us, you know? I know practices can be pretty boring."

"No, I liked it. Josh is pretty entertaining. But you do realize he talks more than he plays."

I laugh. "It's probably better that way."

Her smile widens. "And anyway, I said I wanted to spend this last month with you. And I meant it."

"But you also said you wanted to have fun."

She laughs softly to herself. "This *is* fun. I think you forget sometimes that I spent nearly my entire life with you. I chose to do that, didn't I?"

I lower my head to try and hide my shy grin.

"Okay." I'm not going to argue with her. This is the most time I have had with her since the summer after eighth grade—before high school and volleyball games and guys named Rylan took her away.

"What's this?"

"What?"

I look over at her, and she's eyeing a piece of paper I had *tried* to hide away on a shelf.

"Is this a poem?"

I grab the paper from her hand. "No," I say, my cheeks getting hot again. "It's Shelby's."

"But it's your handwriting."

I look at the page. *Damn it. How can she tell that?*

"It's just something I wrote."

She smiles at me.

"Like a poem?"

I try and sidestep her question, silently thanking God she found that piece of paper after Dillon and Josh had left.

"You wanna go outside...to the dock?" I ask, trying desperately to change the subject.

"Okay."

She says the word hesitantly, but thankfully, she drops the poem thing.

I stand and shove the piece of paper under an empty box, and then I follow her out of the garage and to the dock that's behind my house.

We find a spot at the end, where we can dangle our feet over the side.

The air is a little cool, but it's not too bad.

"I can't believe I'm leaving here."

She's staring off past the water in the lake and into the tree line on the other side.

"I know. It's weird," I say.

"I'm going to have to make all new friends. And the teachers are all going to be different. Everything is going to be different."

I let out a sigh. I don't like talking about her leaving or being gone. I don't know what it's like not having her here. And I definitely can't imagine being in her shoes.

I look over at her. Her lips are turned down at their corners. She looks sad.

"The mountain and the molehill have this in common," I say. "They can be moved."

She laughs.

"Where do you come up with these things?"

I feel my mouth turning up into a grin. "They're floating around in the air. You don't see them?" I act as if I'm pulling something out of the air. "I see one I like, and I just grab it."

She giggles some more. "You're so strange sometimes."

"But yet, you're still here."

She lowers her head but keeps her happy smile.

"But seriously," I say, "what I mean is that getting out of bed, tying your shoes, moving across the country, making new friends—it's all the same. They're all things *you* can do."

I watch her push her lips to one side and then sigh. "I wish you could come with me." She looks up at me.

"To South Carolina?"

She nods.

If she only knew how bad I wanted to jump in that car with her.

"Then who would take care of Rusty?" I ask.

She looks as if she tries to smile, and then she rests her head on my shoulder.

"I'm gonna miss Rusty."

Rusty's a cat we rescued one day from a culvert at the edge of town. He was a kitten then. He lives at my house. I took him because her dad is allergic to cats. But we've both taken care of him for seven years now.

"I'll take good care of him," I say. "I'll feed him his cat food and make sure he always has his cat toys to play with. And maybe, if he's lucky, you'll leave him your cat comforter, so he can have all the purple cat friends he wants."

She laughs and then nestles her cheek deeper into my shoulder. "If he's lucky."

Her laughter fades into the lake water. And the world, all of a sudden, gets smaller, until there's just room enough for me and her.

"Will you tell me one of your poems?" she asks in a soft voice that's barely over a whisper.

I groan, wishing now I had burned that paper.

"Please. It'll make me feel better."

I throw back my head and groan some more.

"The one up at the house. Tell me that one."

I smile, reluctantly, and it comes with a sigh.

"Fine." I grumble out the word, and then I take a deep breath and then let it go. Meanwhile, she lies back against the boards of the dock and stares up into the darkening sky.

"At night," I say but then stop. I feel weird telling her a poem, especially one that I wrote. I only wrote a few. I started writing them a couple months ago. They were supposed to be songs. But even if the band could play a whole song, they're not the type of songs we would ever sing, anyway.

I tried. I tried to write a cool song—one that we could put to music someday. But every time I sat down to do it, I could only think of Vannah. So as it turns out, every word I ever put down on paper was about her. And I know there's no way in hell Dillon or Josh would ever consider playing a love song. So, I never planned for anyone to see them, and I sure as hell never expected to ever be reciting one to *her*. ...But then, I never expected her to ever ask, either. And who knows, maybe it will make her feel better.

"At night," I begin again.

"The girl in the cotton dress
Tiptoes on swaying branch.
Never flown at all.
But not afraid to fall.
For if it breaks,
She'll just spread her wings
And fly."

When I finish, all I can hear are the crickets and the tree frogs, until she breathes. She sounds...content.

"I like that one," she whispers.

The moments grow silent. I look down at her. Her eyes are searching the evening sky. I wonder if she knows the song's about her.

"I've missed this."

"Missed what?" I ask, still watching her face.

"Us."

I smile at that. "Me too."

And in that moment, the air is filled with the sound of the crickets chirping in the sycamores around us and the soft rush of the water pushing against the dock.

"So, what do you want to do with the time you have left here?" I ask.

A few heartbeats drum out a rhythm in my chest, and then I hear her voice.

"I just want to lie here like this...with you and rewind time and play back all the things we did when we were little. And I want to stare off into the sky until it turns black, and I want to soak up every last piece of this place, so I can take it with me. And that's what I want to do."

I keep my stare on her wandering eyes.

Tonight?"

"Every night," she says.

"That's it?"

"That's it," she says, with a nod.

"Okay," I whisper.

She closes her eyes, and I notice the way her smile lingers on her lips. I love that smile on her best. It's her smile for when she's thinking of something happy.

I'm going to miss that smile.

I'm going to miss her.

And right then, I realize that no matter what happens, no matter where life takes her...or me...or us, she'll always be *my* girl...forever.

She's mine—my forever girl. I'll always think of her that way.

Eben: You up?

Vannah: Yep ☺

Eben: I really liked hanging out with you tonight.

Vannah: ☺ Me too! We should do it again.

Eben: Tomorrow?
Vannah: Tomorrow!
Eben: Good night, V
Vannah: Sweet dreams, E

Chapter Nine

Salem
(Sixteen Years Old)

Day 4,023

I pull up to Vannah's house at eight. It's the quickest I could get here. I had more lawns to mow than usual today.

A few months ago, I got in my head that I wanted to start a mowing business. Dad was against it, at first. He wanted me to start working at the lumberyard. But it only took him a day to come around. That next night, he came up to me and said that maybe it was good for me to find out what it's like to run my own business. And that was that. I started cutting grass around town the next day. And it caught on pretty good. Turns out, there are a lot of people around here who'd rather *not* deal with lawn mowers and hedge trimmers. And as it turns out, I don't mind it so much. It's kind of calming, to me.

But today, of all days, I got a call from Coach Hoffman asking me if I could mow his grass. And of course, I can't say *no* to coach. And of course, he's got the biggest and the hilliest damn lawn in Allandale.

I stop my truck, and the first thing I see is her.

She's got a white towel wrapped around her body, her hair is down, and she's not wearing any shoes.

"What are you doing?"

She turns back toward me with her finger to her lips.

"Shh."

I watch her pull the screen door shut like she's closing the door to the Taj Mahal. And then she tiptoes over the wooden porch boards and down the narrow set of stairs.

"Why are you only wearing a towel?" I whisper, loudly.

And at that moment, I can't think of a good reason why I'd ever ask her that question.

"Shh. Turn your lights off."

I quickly push the knob that runs the lights, and instantly, the space around us grows dark.

"What in tarnation are we doing?" I ask her, when she gets closer to the truck.

"I'm supposed to be packing."

She tiptoes in front of the truck, and at the same time, I lean over and open the passenger's side door. And she climbs right in.

"Your parents are gonna have my head."

"Nah." She looks as if she doesn't have a care in her bones. "It'll be fine. Just back out with your lights off."

I stare at her. She's not paying any attention to me anymore. She just keeps stuffing what looks as if it's her clothes into a cloth bag.

This just might be the best or the worst night of my life. Hell, I guess, it could be both.

And with that thought, my mind immediately changes gears.

"Okay," I say, shifting in my seat so I can see out the back window.

My heart is pounding. I let the truck mostly roll back down the hill, and then once I hit the gravel road, I turn the lights back on and quickly step on the gas.

"Where are we going?"

"Hogan's slab?" she both says and asks, at the same time.

"Sounds good."

That's all I say. And after a few moments, she finishes fiddling with her bag and looks up at me.

"You sure no one's going to realize you're gone?"

She shakes her head. "Whitney's talking to her boyfriend in her room. They'll be on the phone all night. And honestly, I haven't seen Mom or Dad for a week now. They've been busy doing whatever it is you do when you move across the country."

"Like pack?"

"Yeah."

"Don't you have to pack?"

I try to conceal my smile.

"I'm already finished."

"Already?"

"Yeah, I stuck it all in four boxes. Two for me.

And two for you."

"For me?"

"Yeah, when I come back, I'm going to need my stuff."

"You're coming back?"

"Eventually," she sighs.

Something in me leaps to life.

"When I turn eighteen, I can do whatever I want," she adds.

I look over at her.

"I'd like that—if you came back."

She smiles at me. And my eyes just rest in her green sea. It's a good moment. But it ends all too soon when the creek comes into view and I pull off to the side of the road and softly tap the brakes.

And as soon as I get the truck turned off, she jumps out and slams the door behind her. And I just watch, motionless, as she dances in that sandy road. Sometimes, I still can't believe she's that same little girl that used to steal all my gummy worms when I wasn't looking.

I follow her with my eyes, until she reaches the edge of the concrete slab and then drops her towel.

Just then, I sit up straight and freeze in my seat.

She's got some kind of little swimsuit bottoms on, but she's not wearing any top.

My breath gets stuck in my throat. I try to swallow, but I can't. And then I sit there for a second, wondering what I should do, until something lights a fire under my ass, and I pull on the door latch and jump out of the truck.

Within seconds, I'm at the slab, just as she's jumping in.

Water splashes up and soaks into my jeans and tee

shirt. And then her head comes back up, and she's rubbing her eyes.

"Come on," she says, staring back up at me.

I don't move. I don't say anything. I just stand there.

She laughs. "Eben, come on."

That's all the coaxing I need. In the next breath, I snap out of my trance, and just like that, I'm kicking off my shoes and pulling off my tee shirt. She watches me as I do it. And as soon as I've got my jeans pulled off, I jump into the water next to her.

Immediately, I suck in a quick breath. The water's ice cold. "What are we doing?" I laugh through my pain.

"Skinny dipping," she says. "I always wanted to try it."

"But we're not..."

She holds up a tiny pair of swimsuit bottoms.

I feel my eyes grow wide.

"Savannah Catesby, you're gonna kill me yet."

She tosses the bottoms, and they land on the slab. And then she gives me a prodding look.

"Okay," I say.

I take off my boxers and throw them onto the slab, too. I'm happy, for my sake, this old creek water is kind of murky, but then again, looking at her, I also wish it weren't.

I smile at her, and she gives me a proud look back.

I can't help but laugh at that.

"Girl, it is sixty-five degrees, and this water's even colder. You couldn't have picked to do this in July?"

She laughs, and her voice carries over the water and lingers in the misty air.

"But I won't be here in July."

My smile starts to fade, but hers stays.

"Are you cold?" she asks.

"Yeah, hell yeah, I'm cold."

"You wanna get out?"

That's a trick question. Half of me wants to get the hell out of this freezing water and put my dry clothes back on, but the other half realizes that I'm also next to Savannah Catesby, and she just so happens to be...naked.

"I'm getting out," she says.

"What?" I laugh. "Already?"

"It's freezing in here," she screams.

I watch, with a smile on my face, as she swims to her towel and climbs out of the water. She's pretty crafty at getting that towel around her so fast, but I do manage to steal a quick glance at her upper thigh before she's all covered up.

"I brought you a towel, too," she says, turning my way.

I quickly drop my gaze before finding hers again.

She just gives me a playful, scolding look, before she grabs her little cloth bag and pulls out a towel.

"Here," she says, holding it out to me, "unlike yourself, I won't look."

I try to hide my mischievous smile, as she turns her face. I'd hesitate, but it's too damn cold to be self-conscious.

I pull myself back up onto the concrete slab and wrap the towel around my waist.

And then she faces me again and lets out a soft, desperate scream. "I'm so cold," she squeals, crossing her arms against her chest. "I feel like a human Popsicle."

I laugh. She looks so cute. Her hair is slicked back,

and there are little beads of water on her long eyelashes.

"But you're a cute little human Popsicle, at least."

She shivers some more.

"Here," I say. I walk over to her and wrap my arms around her. She lets me do it, but she keeps her arms crossed over her chest. And she probably doesn't even think anything of it, but feeling her warm skin against mine makes me think back to when we were kids and arm wrestling and playing Red Rover and all those thumb wars. Her skin on mine didn't matter a hill of beans back then. But now...it makes my senses come alive.

She squeals, as she shivers some more. I squeeze her tighter. And then, she grows quiet. And I hold her there for a few more long, silent moments, until her eyes travel up to mine.

She's got a smile on her face. I want to kiss her. And something tells me she'd kiss me back.

"Um."

I hear her voice, and I loosen my hold on her.

"Maybe we should get dressed," she says.

I can tell she's nervous. I've known Vannah too long not to know what she's feeling.

My heart sinks a little in my chest.

"Yeah," I agree. "Maybe."

She walks over to her bag and pulls out some dry clothes. And then she turns back to me.

"Can you, uh, maybe turn that way?" she asks, pointing behind me.

"Uh, yeah, of course."

I turn around and go to my boxers and jeans and tee shirt, which are strewn about the concrete. And as she puts her clothes back on, I shake out the sand and throw on mine, too.

And when I turn around again, she's sitting on the edge of the slab—fully clothed—dangling her feet over the side.

I press the towel to my head and rub it into my hair, and then I take a seat beside her.

"Do you see how the moon makes the water light up?" she asks.

I look at the creek water and notice the moonlight reflecting off of it.

I nod. "I do."

She keeps her eyes on that light, so I do, too.

"That's why I like it here," she says.

I take my eyes off the water, and instead, focus on her. She's got this look in her eyes. And if you didn't know her, you'd probably guess it were wonder. But I know it's something more like *wander*, instead. Her mind is wandering...through tunnels and caves and old, abandoned sheds we used to find out near my house when we were little. And if I had to guess, I'd guess it was also wandering through the future...through times we haven't even had yet.

"I'm guessing you've been here before, at night, I mean?" I ask, breaking her silence.

I force my eyes back to the creek water, but I can feel hers on me.

"I have," she says, softly, returning her attention to the moonlight.

"I'm just going to pretend it wasn't with *him*."

I feel her eyes on me again, and this time, I look at her.

"Okay," she whispers. A roguish smile stretches across her face.

"Vannah, did you like him?"

She breathes in, holds the breath in her lungs for a

few beats and then forces it out.

"I did."

I nod. "But I mean, did you really like him?"

She presses her hands against the concrete slab and leans back.

"I thought I did." There's a pause, and the air between us grows thick. "But maybe I didn't."

I try to conceal my thankful sigh by bringing my fist to my mouth.

"Because I didn't want to spend my last month here with him," she adds.

Her words hit my ears and somehow melt my heart. And even after it turns quiet, I just keep replaying her last sentence in my head, until a question takes hold of my thoughts and won't let go.

"Why do you call me *Eben*?"

She meets my gaze, and a smile starts to crawl across her sun-tanned face. "For Ebenezer."

"No, I mean, but why not just call me Salem?"

"Because everyone needs a nickname."

I push my cheek out with my tongue while I try not to smile. "But you've never called anyone but me by another name."

Her head spins back toward me. There's a look of surprise or shock or awe on her face—I can't tell which.

"What? That's not true."

I shrug. "Not your sister. Not Tracy. Not Julain. Not Lindsay. Not even *him*."

I watch her eyebrows knit together, as her attention goes back to that moonlight creeping up the creek.

She's quiet for almost a whole minute.

"I...," she starts but then stops. "I don't know why I call you Eben."

She looks back at me with a wide smile on her face. "And I don't know how you know that no one else has a nickname."

"Vannah." I sit back and laugh. "I've been right here by your side all your life. Why wouldn't I know that?"

Her top teeth press into her bottom lip, but she still doesn't say a word.

"Well, why do *you* think I call you Eben?"

I look down at our feet and think about it.

"I think it's because you like me."

She finds my eyes.

"Salem Ebenezer!"

She pushes her shoulder into mine and then smiles and falls back against the concrete.

I carefully let a breath escape my lungs, and then I look back at her when she doesn't sit back up. Her focus is on that black sky now, and she's just smiling away.

We've been friends for a long time. And I know that's hard to break. I just wonder if she'll ever be able to see past it.

"Look at the stars with me," she says, never taking her eyes off the sky.

I lean back, and after tossing a small rock out of the way, I fold my hands under my head and look up, too.

"You have two choices," she says.

"Okay."

"You can fly to the moon and see the stars up close, and you can look down and see the whole world and all its oceans and lights and people..."

Her words trail off.

"But?" I ask.

"But," she starts, "you can't come back."

"Or?" I ask.

"Or, you can stay right here."

I smile. "That's easy."

She turns her face my way.

"I'd stay right here," I say.

"But you could see the world, literally."

I shrug it off. She's my world, but of course, those words never leave my mouth.

"Here is just fine," I say, instead.

She looks at me with a half-questioning look, and then she leans my way and rests her head on my chest.

I almost stop breathing. I wasn't expecting that. I try to calm myself as she wraps her arm around me.

"I'm glad you always forgot your lunch," she whispers.

I smile into the gentle breeze. "I'm glad you always brought yours."

I hear her laugh softly, as she nuzzles more into my chest. And I pray that she doesn't hear my wild heartbeat. And I pray, too, that that full moon has a hard time finding the sun on the other side of the world—because I'm okay with this night lasting a little while longer.

Eben: You awake?

Vannah: Yep

Eben: Did you get in trouble with your parents?

Vannah: No. They didn't even notice.

Eben: How? It's 3 a.m.!

Vannah: I said I was with you.

Eben: I don't know how I'm supposed to feel about that.

Vannah: Oh, don't worry. They still think you're sexy. They just trust you.

Eben: That's weird.

Vannah: Lol!

Vannah: I had fun tonight.

Eben: Me too.

Vannah: I can't sleep. Will you tell me a story??

Eben: About what?

Vannah: Anything

Eben: Okay

Eben: Once upon a time, there was this boy, and one day, he met this beautiful girl, with long blond hair and a pretty nice butt.

Vannah: ☺

Eben: And turns out, this girl could grant one wish to the boy.

Vannah: A wish-granting girl? Like a genie?

Eben: Yeah. But just one wish. Not three.

Vannah: Eben??

Eben: To be continued...

Vannah: Okay, fine! Good night, E.

Eben: Sweet dreams, V.

Chapter Ten

Savannah
(Sixteen Years Old)

Day 4,028

"Eben."

I tap on his window. The room is completely dark, and his blinds are closed. I can't see anything.

"Eben," I whisper. I tap some more.

All of a sudden, the blinds lift, and there's a dark figure in the window.

"Vannah?"

"Shh."

"What are you doing?" He acts as if he's whispering this time, but I can't really hear him. I can only read his lips.

"Hold on," he mouths.

He leaves the window, and a few moments later, I hear his front door squeak open.

I shimmy out of the peony bushes and head to the front porch. But I stop when I see him.

He's just standing there. He's barefoot, shirtless. The only thing clinging to his skin is an old pair of black sweatpants.

"What are you doing?" he asks.

His laughter breaks my concentration on his shirtless self. And I must be giving him a funny look because now he's wearing a playful smile.

"What?"

"You're cute." I just say it, matter-of-fact.

He smiles. It's bashful, but I expected that.

"Okay...thanks?"

I nod and smile, too.

"Vannah, it's midnight."

"Yeah, but it's Saturday."

He seems to think about it and then nods. "Okay, yeah, you've got a point."

We stand there for a moment, staring at each other. I think he's waiting on me to tell him the plan for tonight. But I don't really have a plan. And the longer we stand here, the more I think he realizes that.

"Come to the dock with me."

He lowers his head. I can tell he's trying not to laugh. "All right."

He turns back and closes the door and then makes his way down the porch steps, still barefoot, still shirtless.

"Do you really think I'm cute?"

I nod. "Yeah. I think so."

His soft chuckle fills the space between us.

"You *think* so?"

"I know so."

I laugh, partially because he has this new air of confidence, all of a sudden.

"I mean, I see you every day, and I see...you," I say. "I just think I rarely stop to see what body you're in."

"So, I'm in a good body?"

"Yeah. You're in a good body."

He smiles proudly.

We get to the dock and walk to the end of it, and then we both just stop and stare out into the water.

"You think they'll have docks like this in South Carolina?"

He nods. "Yeah, I reckon they do. Only instead of lakes, they've got an ocean. So, it'll be better than this dock."

I look up at him. "I don't think so."

I sit down and dangle my feet off the edge, and seconds later, he does, too.

"I don't think anything can be better than this," I say.

The water is dark, like black diamonds, glistening in the moonlight.

"Plus, there are no Ebens on those boat docks in South Carolina."

He smiles. "You don't think?"

"Probably not," I say, shaking my head.

"You could always stay. You could stay here...with me. You know, Mom wouldn't mind."

"I know, but mine would. I've got to go, Eben."

He lets out a long, defeated sigh. "I know. I know you do."

I find his eyes. They're warm and light. They feel like sunrays and look like the color of sand. And the way he's looking at me now, I know he wants to kiss me. I can see it, but more so, I can feel it. And I want to kiss him back. But where would that leave us?

I feel a little piece of my heart tearing for us...for him...for me. I've always had a thing for Salem Ebenezer. But when I was little, I didn't know what it meant, and when I was old enough to know what it meant, I feared he didn't feel the same way. And now... And now, it doesn't matter anymore.

He puts his arm around me, and I breathe in the smell of his bedsheets. I'm going to miss the smell of his bed...and his room—his dumb, boy room, with its old Spiderman comforter and drum set and boy things. It reminds me of all those long nights we would spend holed up in there, eating chicken and dumplings and trying to make it across the Oregon Trail without one of us getting dysentery.

I'm going to miss it all. But mostly, I'm going to miss him.

I love him.

I always have.

Vannah: Thanks for walking me home.
Eben: Thanks for rescuing my Saturday night.
Vannah: ☺
Vannah: Can you tell me some more of the story?
Eben: Okay
Eben: So, the boy thought about what he wanted his one wish to be. There were so many things he wanted: a dirt bike, a four-wheeler, a new lawn mower. Hell, maybe even wings to fly or superhuman strength

or x-ray vision.

Vannah: What would he use x-ray vision for?

Eben: Don't worry about it.

Vannah: Lol!

Eben: Anyway, he thought real hard about it, and then it came to him.

Vannah: What did he pick?

Eben: To be continued...

Vannah: Eben!

Eben: Good night, V.

Vannah: Sweet dreams, E.

Chapter Eleven

Salem
(Sixteen Years Old)

Day 4,039

"**Y**ou leave tomorrow."

We're at Hogan's slab, just standing on the cool concrete, side by side, staring at that big moon.

"No," she says.

"No what?"

"No, I don't leave."

I give her a confused look, but something inside me also springs to life.

"I've decided I'm going to stay here. I'm just going to disappear into the wind and stay here forever."

My chest deflates, as I chuckle softly and take her hand.

The action throws her off, I can tell.

I just figure that if she can put her head on my chest, then I can hold her hand. And plus, I feel as if I'm losing her. I feel as if I'm losing control. And the more time I spend with her, the more I think the boundary between friends and *more* starts to blur.

Her head is lowered. Her focus is on her hand, now intertwined with mine. I like the way her hand feels, but mostly, I like the way it makes me feel—like I could float away if I weren't tethered to her.

After a few heartbeats, she looks up. She's breathtaking. I've never said that about someone...or even thought that about anyone. But that's the only word that fits. *Breathtaking*.

Her eyes catch on mine. I study the greens, the golds, the browns that swirl around her thoughts. It's as if they're pulling me in.

She doesn't move. She just keeps her wandering stare in mine. My breaths quicken. My heart beats faster and faster.

I move my face closer to hers. She doesn't move away.

I move in even closer, and just like that, our lips are touching.

An electric shock zings through my body.

I move my mouth over hers. She doesn't pull away. In fact, she does the same. Adrenaline shoots through my core and out to my limbs.

They're just a few moments—a few, crazy moments of untamed emotion, and then our lips part. But those few moments just might have been the best few moments of my life.

She's staring into my eyes. I'm too damn happy to be terrified, but my mind is telling me that maybe I should be...a little.

"What was that?" she asks.

She sounds nervous, maybe even a little panicked.

"A kiss," I mumble, hoarsely.

My heart starts to race again. I don't want her to run. She looks as if she's going to run. A second goes by, then two, then three.

"Okay," she whispers.

And the space between us grows silent. And then something changes in her eyes. It's as if fear is replaced with desire. And I can't help but be drawn to her.

I rest my hand on the back of her head and then pause before pulling her close.

Our lips touch, and it's even better than the first time—if that's possible. This time, her lips are hungry, as if this dance is something she had longed for—just as much as I had longed for her. It's a slow burn, mixed with love and want and passion—eleven years in the making.

And then, it's over. And she presses her forehead to mine.

"Vannah." I take a quick breath. "I could really get used to this."

She smiles softly.

"Don't," she whispers.

Her sad word brings me back down to earth.

"We're just friends," she says, shaking her head.

I pull away from her but keep my hands resting on her shoulders. There's this uncertainty on her face. It makes me think she doesn't even believe what she's saying.

"And I leave tomorrow," she adds.

She looks down at the concrete before finding my eyes again. I wish I could make her see what I see—that what we were and where we'll be doesn't matter.

I sigh inwardly and wrap my arms around her. My heart aches for her—for her time, for her kiss, for moments like this I might never get again. I think it's all kind of just hitting me now.

Her head rests on my chest. I can hear her breathe in and then slowly breathe out, as the seconds fall away into the soft breeze.

It's dark out. There's a smell of honeysuckle in the air. I can hear the creek water softly moving through the big piece of concrete under our feet.

For a few, perfect seconds, her head presses against my heart. And I feel as if she's mine—mine to hold, mine to love. Then, without warning, she steps back, forcing my arms from around her.

I watch her, as she walks backwards a couple steps, keeping her gaze on me. And if I'm not mistaken, there are tears in her eyes. Then suddenly, she stops and lowers herself to the edge of the slab.

"You coming?" She looks back at me but then turns before I can answer. And in her next move, she's lying back against the chipped and weathered concrete.

My heart is still pounding, but somehow, I manage to convince my body to move toward her.

"Here," I say, pulling off my tee shirt.

She looks up at me. It wasn't really my intention, but her stare lingers on my midsection.

"It's okay. I'm fine."

"No, just take it. I'm hot anyway."

She gives me a playful smile, and then she takes the shirt. I watch her fold it into threes and then position it under her head.

"Here," she says, patting one side of the tee shirt, "there's enough room for two."

I look at the little piece of cloth next to her head, and without hesitation, I press my back against the hard concrete and lay my head next to hers.

"Eben?"

"Yeah?"

"What do you want to be when you grow up?"

I take a breath and then force it out.

"Well, my dad's hell-bent on handing down the lumberyard to me."

Out of the corner of my eye, I can see her head bob.

"Are you hell-bent on taking it?"

I laugh. "Yeah," I say, nodding. "I wouldn't mind taking it over someday. It's been in the family for years."

She breathes out a smile.

"Maybe I'll work for the *Times*."

"*The New York Times*?"

"Yeah."

"All the way in New York?"

"Maybe," she says.

We both sit there then, listening to the water soothingly make its way from one side of the slab to the other.

"I'm gonna call you...after you're gone," I say, breaking the sweet silence.

"I know," she says.

I reach for her hand, and she lets me hold it.

And I just smile. My heart's breaking, but I smile anyway because despite what tomorrow brings, I still have her tonight.

And I don't know how much time goes by before

we both drift off to sleep, our sides touching, her hand in mine—maybe for one, last time.

Vannah: You get home okay?
Eben: Safe and sound.
Vannah: ☺ Good.
Eben: I had fun tonight.
Vannah: Me too.
Eben: When do you leave?
Vannah: In about 5 hours.
Eben: ☹
Vannah: You still haven't finished the story.
Eben: Oh, yeah
Vannah: What does the boy wish for? My bet's on the x-ray vision.
Eben: Haha!
Eben: His wish is for the girl.
Vannah: So he can have all the wishes he wants?
Eben: Yeah. Something like that. ;)
Vannah: Eben
Eben: Yeah
Vannah: I'd stay if I could.
Eben: I know
Eben: I'm going to miss you.
Vannah: I already miss you.
Eben: You should get some sleep.
Vannah: Probably
Eben: Don't stay away forever.
Vannah: I won't.
Eben: Promise?
Vannah: Promise

Eben: Good night, V
Vannah: Sweet dreams, E

Chapter Twelve

Salem
(Sixteen Years Old)

Day 4,041

It's the 2nd of October, and it's the first day that Savannah isn't at her usual spot in the hallway before school.

I look around to make sure no one is looking, and I open her locker door, just to see if she's really gone.

Inside, the shelves are empty—no books, no pictures of her or her friends or Rusty, no bag, no sign of Vannah. But then I see a little folded up piece of paper sitting on the shelf, and I quickly snatch it up.

I start to unfold it, guessing it's probably just some

old note to a friend or a schedule of some kind or something like that, when I stop.

I see my name, and my heart jumps. And my eyes immediately go to reading the rest:

I knew you'd go snooping around my locker after I was gone. I should have left some sort of booby trap!

Anyway, I just wanted to say that I already miss you. This last month was the best month of my life. It stinks it had to end.

You're my favorite person.

Love,
Vannah

P.S. You better tell me when you find my star tower.

P.P.S. The gift is for Rusty. And by Rusty, I mean you. I needed a new one anyway. ☺

Gift?

The locker is empty.

I furrow my brow and close the door. Then I carefully fold the note, stick it deep into my pocket and open the locker right next to hers.

And then I see it.

Stuffed at the very bottom of my locker is a bed comforter—one with little purple cats all over it.

We talked on the phone that whole semester after that. We talked about our days, about Rusty, about her new life in South Carolina and our old life we used to have back here. And then as the winter drew on, we talked less and less. She got a job babysitting for a wealthy couple on some place called Rainbow Row down there, and it snowed here just enough to keep me knee-deep in the snow-removal business—the winter business in the grass business. And then one day, I don't know how or why I noticed it just then, but in the middle of a basketball practice the next year, it just hit me: I hadn't really talked to Vannah for months.

I remember feeling lost in that moment, like someone had just punched me in the gut and left me in some strange place.

I figured she was living her life. The occasional *How are you?* text was nice, but it wasn't quite the same as hearing her voice.

I missed her voice. In fact, I vowed I'd never forget her voice. Every day, I'd replay her saying my name in my head. I think I figured that if I always had her voice, I always had her.

I wish that were true.

Chapter Thirteen

Salem
(Seventeen Years Old)

Day 4,562

"**D**ude, have you heard?"

"Heard what?" I ask, going up for a layup.

"Savannah Catesby is coming back."

"What?" I grab the ball and look back at him. All of a sudden, Dillon Denhammer has my full attention—for the first time...probably ever.

"Savannah? You remember her?" he asks. "Tall. Blond. Played volleyball. Oh, yeah, and you were in love with her."

"Cut the crap, Dillon." I mindlessly squeeze the basketball and then turn it over in my hands. I can feel my legs going numb, but I try not to look as anxious as I feel. "Why is she back?"

Dillon shrugs. "I don't know. But I think it's just for the summer. I overheard her uncle talking about fixing up a room for her."

"No shit," I mumble.

"Yeah, no shit." He laughs and gives me a dumb look, as if he's amused by me or something. "Now, give me the ball."

Without another thought, I throw him the ball. He takes it, dribbles and makes an unsuccessful attempt at a dunk.

"When?"

"What?" He straightens up and looks back at me.

"When will she be here?" I ask, a little louder, this time.

He shrugs again. "I don't know. She might already be here."

I grab the back of my neck and let out an unsteady breath of air. "You know, I just remembered I had something to do tonight."

Dillon eyes me suspiciously. "Yeah," he says, rolling his eyes, "like go find a girl."

I smile and shake my head. "Yeah, something like that."

"Fine, dude, bail on me for a girl." He reaches for the ball near the curb.

"Yeah, that's exactly what I'm going to do." I laugh. "As if this weren't the twenty-ninth night in a row we've done this same thing."

"Yeah, yeah," he says, taking a shot. "But I better see you tomorrow."

"Yeah," I say, "don't count on it."

Chapter Fourteen

Salem
(Seventeen Years Old)

Day 4,562

It's pitch-black outside when I pull up to Lester Klein's house. I turn off the truck first and then its lights, and then I sit there and stare at that old, off-white garage door.

"Damn it, I must be crazy."

I'm just about to start my truck up again and get the hell out of here when the porch lights up.

My pulse starts racing. Her uncle is going to kill me or commit me or something; I just know it.

I hold my breath and watch as the screen door

opens and out steps a girl in gray sweatpants and a dark tee shirt.

I watch, motionless, as she makes her way out onto the porch and squints her eyes at my truck.

"Eben?"

Well, here goes nothin'.

I smile, slowly reach for the door handle and then step out onto the little, pea-size gravel.

"Eben, what are you doing here?"

I shrug and softly close the door behind me.

"I heard you were back in town..."

"Come here," she says, stopping me. "Come up here."

I want to run to her, but I think that might look just a little too crazy. So instead, I calmly make my way up the stone walk and then up the three wooden porch stairs. And before I know it, I'm standing right in front of Savannah Catesby once again—not having the slightest idea of what to say.

"Wow, you look good, Eben." She breathes out a smile. "You're taller."

I bow my head. "Yeah, it's what a growth spurt will do for ya."

"Wow," she says again.

We stand there just like that, staring at each other for what feels like the duration of a *Star Wars* movie. And then she takes a step toward me.

"Well, come here, give me a hug."

She throws her arms around my neck and falls against my chest while I wrap my arms around her. She feels just as good as she smells. I breathe her in, and my senses fill with the sweet, familiar scent of her perfume, laundry soap and that vanilla-scented lotion she always wears.

"Wow, I didn't realize how much I missed you." Her voice is muffled in my chest.

I want to say I missed her, too, but I'm afraid my voice might crack before I get it all out.

"But it looks as if time has been good to you," she says, pulling away from me.

She smiles and then walks over to the porch swing. "Come on, sit down with me."

"Okay," I say, slowly bobbing my head.

I take the couple steps toward the swing and then sit down. I make sure there's some, but not too much, space in between us.

"So, how'd you know I was back?"

"Oh, Dillon overheard your uncle talking about you."

"Aah," she says, nodding her head.

"How come you didn't tell me you were coming back?"

"I wanted to surprise you. I was going to go tap on your window in the middle of the night."

I can't help but smile at that. "I probably would have liked that."

She laughs now, too, and it reminds me of how much I missed her laugh.

"Well, are you back for good?" I ask, when our laughter grows faint.

"No, just for the summer. I'm helping Uncle Lester out at the paper. But mostly, we're just spending time together. That's what Mom said anyway."

I reach for her hand. I don't know why I do it. I just saw her hand, and I felt like holding it. But just as quickly as my skin touches hers, she pulls her hand back.

"Eben."

"What?"

"I have a boyfriend."

My forehead wrinkles, and my heart sinks deep inside my chest.

"You do?"

She nods once. And slowly, my eyes find the floor. I don't want to give away to her what I'm thinking. But after a little while, I can tell she's looking at me. So, I give in and look at her.

"But you're my friend, and that's never gonna change," she says.

My gaze goes straight back down to those weathered boards. Maybe, subconsciously, I'm looking for my heart down there.

"Eben?"

She's silent after that, and I know she wants me to look at her.

"Yeah?" I finally ask, lifting my eyes.

"Can we just pretend I never said the *boyfriend* part? Can we just be *us*?"

"Do I have a choice?"

Somehow, a small smile finds my face. And at the same time, her expression softens.

"Who is he?"

She lets out a sigh, and then she rests her head on my shoulder. "His name is Aaron."

Aaron. I try not to roll my eyes, or at least, not let her catch me doing it. I don't know why it's worse when *they* have a name.

"He plays football. And he's good at it. But he also has a level head, you know?"

I nod, habitually, but I don't care what kind of head this guy's got.

"Are you happy?"

She tilts her face and finds my eyes.

"Yeah," she says, nodding against my shoulder. "I am."

"Okay." I take a breath in and then force it out slowly. "Well, it's getting late. I just wanted to see you with my own eyes."

"Come back tomorrow night."

Something makes me hesitate, but I also know, without a doubt, I'll be back here tomorrow no matter if she's got six boyfriends.

"Okay," I say. And then I stand, refit my baseball cap back over my head and make my way back to my truck.

"Eben."

I turn back toward her.

"You find my star tower yet?"

I chuckle softly to myself.

"Getting close."

"Good," she says, smiling her same, sweet, comfortable smile back at me.

Chapter Fifteen

Salem
(Seventeen Years Old)

Day 4,563

I pull up to Vannah's uncle's house the very next evening—just like I said I would.

I knock on the door, and after a few moments, Lester's standing in front of me with the door wide open.

It seems as if each time I see him, he's getting older and thinner. But still, his hard jaw and easy smile remain unchanged.

"Salem. Come in."

He turns, and I follow him into the little

farmhouse, taking my cap off as I do.

I know Vannah's Uncle Lester. On top of me always hanging around his office with Vannah when we were growing up, he just interviewed me for the basketball story he ran in the paper last week. But it is a little weird being in his house. It's as if I'm invading his personal space or something.

The house is small—one floor, maybe only two bedrooms, and not much is on the walls. Stacks of paper fill several corners, and I can't help but notice the yellow surrounding the landline phone and covering the refrigerator. It's as if he went to war with a pad of sticky notes, and the sticky notes won. In fact, it looks a lot like his newspaper office—just in house form.

Vannah's uncle never married. Everybody always said it was because he married his job. He's owned the only paper in town for as long as I've been alive.

"Savannah's in her room. Says she'll be out in a minute. Why don't you go ahead and take a seat."

"All right." I look around the living room for a place to sit down. All the surfaces seem to be occupied by paper.

Eventually, though, I find an older, leather chair with just this week's newspaper lying on it, and I pick up the paper and sit down.

"You know, I remember you and Savannah playing out behind the paper when you were only yea tall." He holds his hand parallel to the floor, about waist-high.

I lower my head and laugh to myself. "Yeah, I remember that, too."

He looks at me then, like he wants to say something or he's waiting for me to say something or something, so I just start talking.

"This is a nice place."

"Yeah," he says, looking around. "It suits me. Been in the family for a long time."

I nod and notice a photo sitting on a table in the corner of the room. It's of a guy and a girl. The guy looks as if he could be Lester—a young Lester with dark, shaggy hair and black-rimmed glasses. But I don't recognize the girl.

"Olivia," he says, catching me off guard.

"Sir?"

"The girl in the photo. It's Olivia Ryan."

"Oh," I say, not really knowing what to say next.

He sighs and walks over to the little table.

"You know how they say we all have that one great love in our lives?"

I'm not sure if he wants me to answer, but he's awful quiet after that, so I just do.

"I...I guess," I stutter.

He smiles.

"Well, she was mine."

And if I didn't know what to say a minute ago, I sure as hell don't know what to say now. So, I just watch him as he picks up the frame and touches the photo, like he's wishing he could bring it to life or something.

"What happened to her?" And maybe I shouldn't have asked, but it was quiet, and I don't know what to do with the quiet sometimes.

He sighs and sets the frame back down onto the little table. "She married some guy, moved to Colorado and had two children."

It doesn't sound like a sad story. I was bracing myself for something tragic, like a car accident or some illness. Even so, the story sounds sad, coming from him.

"I'm sorry," I say.

"No." He shakes his head. "My own damn fault. You live. You learn, huh?"

He glances up at me, and I nod, slowly. "I imagine that's right."

I watch him then as he walks back over to the chair across from me, picks up a stack of papers and takes a seat.

"You're wearing a chain," he says, pointing to my chest.

I look down and notice the key dangling from my neck. I immediately feel embarrassed. I always keep it tucked inside my shirt.

"Yeah," I say, trying to get it back where it belongs.

"It got any significance?"

He's nosy, but I guess I probably should have expected that, coming into a newspaper guy's house.

"Nah. Not really."

He nods his head and makes a face like he's satisfied enough with my answer, but I can't imagine he is.

"Eben."

Vannah comes into the room, instantly halting our conversation.

I stand up. I don't know what makes me do it; I just do. And I get a good look at her, although I try to be subtle about it. It's as if she grew up over night. She looks different somehow. She's got on painted-on jeans and a black tee shirt tied at her waist. The shirt has a V-necked collar, and she's wearing a gold necklace that doesn't end before the shirt begins. I swallow and try not to give away to anybody—especially her uncle— that I'd like to see where that gold chain leads.

"You ready?" she asks.

"Yeah," I say, refitting my cap back over my head.

"Take care of her," Lester says, holding out his hand.

I meet his with mine. He squeezes my hand harder than his usual handshake, and I can tell he makes sure to look me in the eye, until I feel uncomfortable.

"I will," I promise him.

"Oh, come on," Vannah says, grabbing my arm. "We're just going down the way."

Vannah drags me to the door and then turns back.

"I'll be back soon, Uncle Les."

Lester looks down at the floor briefly and then returns with a smile on his face. "You guys have fun."

I notice Vannah smile back at him, right before she pulls me out the door.

And once we're out on the porch, she stops and eyes me up and down.

"You look nice."

I feel my cheeks growing a little hot. "Thanks. You...uh, you look grown up."

She gives me a sideways smile. It makes me laugh.

"It looks good on you," I add.

She bites her bottom lip and then takes the few steps down to the stone walk. "Thanks," she says, turning back toward me.

The edges of my mouth slowly curve up, and after a moment of just standing there, trying to convince myself she's real and that she's really here, I follow after her.

"So, what were you guys talking about?"

"Oh. Just stuff."

She nods, seemingly satisfied with my answer.

"Your uncle's pretty cool."

"Yeah, he is."

She stops in front of the passenger's door.

"Still got it, huh?"

She's looking at my truck.

"Yep, never sellin' her."

I open her door for her, and not only because it's the right thing to do, but also because the damn thumb button is as hard as hell to get down. Vannah knows this, which is also why she never even tries.

I step back, and she climbs right in. And I gently close the door behind her.

"So, where are we headed?" I ask, once I get behind the wheel.

"I want to see the moon." She smiles out the passenger's window.

"Okay," I whisper.

That's all I say. And we head toward Hogan's slab.

"**T**ake me back, Eben."

We're sitting on the slab, dangling our legs over the edge. The concrete is warm, and the sound of the water pushing underneath the slab is filling the air around us.

"Back?"

"Yeah," she says, sticking little white wildflowers into her hair, "to when we could change it all. Rewind time. Make me see that I liked you at eleven, twelve, thirteen. Make me tell you that I liked you under those stairs that day that you chickened out."

"What?"

She turns to me. "I knew, Eben. I knew that's what you were going to say."

I lower my eyes and smile, letting seconds fall to

the water under our feet. I don't know whether to be shocked or embarrassed.

"Why didn't you say anything?"

"I don't know." She shrugs. "I didn't know if you had changed your mind at the last second. I figured if you liked me enough, you'd tell me, eventually."

"Wait. You liked me?"

She smiles and looks my way. "The ham and cheese sandwiches didn't give it away?"

I feel my jaw go slack, as my mouth hangs open.

"Vannah, this whole time... Are you telling me this whole time, we could have been together? Like really been together?"

She shrugs.

I feel a breath escape my lungs as I refit my Cardinals cap over my head.

"But why can't we now?"

"I don't know, Eben." She breathes out a sigh and goes to picking at a tear in her jeans. "For starters, I have a boyfriend."

I let go of a puff of air. I hate that she brings up the boyfriend.

"And I'm still a thousand miles from where you are," she adds.

I go to gnawing on the inside of my cheek. I think it's a nervous habit.

"I really do like Aaron. And he lives in the same part of the world." She smiles. "That's a plus."

"But what about when you turn eighteen? You could come back then."

She exhales, but she keeps her stare on that moonlight, reflecting off the water as if it's little pieces of broken glass. "I thought about it. And I'm not sure how I'll feel in a year, but..."

I already know I'm not going to like the rest of this story.

"But I think I might stay and go to college there, maybe. My dad said the in-state tuition would be a good thing."

She briefly looks up at me.

"Well, I could go there. After I graduate, I could go to South Carolina."

She shifts her face, so that her eyes are in mine. And a piece of her long hair falls from her shoulders and comes to rest on her chest.

"What about the lumberyard?"

I feel my lungs fill with air. She's right. I don't want to say it, but she's right. I know I'm the next in line. I've already closed up shop on my lawn-cutting business, just so I can start learning my way around the lumberyard again.

She rests her head on my shoulder. "Have you ever thought that maybe the universe just doesn't want us together? That maybe that's why it made us friends?"

I sigh. I don't know what to say. What do you say when you're coming to terms with the fact that you might have missed your chance...for good? Or that maybe you never even had a chance at all?

"Do you remember when we were in fourth grade, and we did that play?"

I know she's trying to change the subject, but I don't even have the heart to fight her on it.

"What was it?" she asks.

I stare off into the water and think about it for a second.

"*Pocahontas*," I finally say.

"Yeah." I can hear the smile in her voice.

"You forgot your lines," I say.

"And you said them for me."

Her head is still on my shoulder, but I know she's looking up at me.

"'It would've been better if we had never met,'" I recite the line. "'None of this would've happened.'"

The irony isn't lost on me, and she seems to notice, too.

She nestles her cheek more into my shoulder. "Those were the words."

I don't say anything.

"You were manning the curtains off stage, weren't you?" she asks.

I feel a small smile start to cultivate on my face as I think back. "I was."

"And no one ever questioned the voice from above," she says, dramatically raising her hand.

"No one was the wiser," I agree.

"I was," she says, turning her face up toward mine.

I catch her stare. And as if it's pure instinct, I put my arm around her.

She stiffens a little.

"I know. I know," I say. "The boyfriend."

I feel her body relax.

"We're friends, though, right?"

She breathes out a smile. "Right."

It's quiet then, until a memory rushes into my head like a freight train, drowning everything else out.

"The day after that play, I got my first shiner," I say.

"Oh, that's right. The hockey puck."

"Yeah."

"I got you ice from the cafeteria."

"No," I say, chuckling under my breath. "The ice melted before you got to me. You brought me your cold hands, instead, and held them to my eye until the nurse came."

There's a surprised look on her face, until something new washes over her. "That's right. I couldn't find a bag to put the ice in."

I shrug. "It was fine. Your hands were nice."

She looks at me and smiles before reaching for my hand. And I must look a little shocked because her next words come out in a scolding tone.

"Friends can hold hands."

I don't argue. Meanwhile, the tree frogs surrounding us begin their nightly chirps. And I watch as several stars start to pop out of the black background. And the whole time, there's this comfortable hush between us. I think we're both just gnawing on pieces of our past—long gone.

"Vannah," I say, after a little while.

"Hmm?"

"You're a bird on a windowsill."

I hear her grin.

"I'm a what?"

"A bird," I say. "You're there one second, and the next, you're gone. But every time I see you there, I can't help but stop and look at you."

She's quiet, but that water just keeps pushing a path beneath us, making a soft, whooshing sound.

"Eben?"

"Mm hmm?"

"Are you trying to tell me I'm pretty?"

I shake my head. "No. I'm trying to tell you that you're the most intriguing...and the most captivating...and the most beautiful bird I've ever seen."

She looks up at me and rests her gaze in my eyes. She almost looks as if she's searching me, looking for

98

something she hasn't found in the last twelve years we've known each other.

"You mean that."

"Of course I do," I say, even though what she said wasn't a question.

She lays her head back on my shoulder and squeezes my hand.

"Do you have to go back?"

I don't know why I ask it. I already know she does.

Even so, she moves her head back and forth. "Not now."

"Ever?"

She doesn't say anything.

"I mean, I *can* come this time. I can finish high school there, and I don't have to do the lumberyard business. I mean, my dad can run it for a long time, still."

"Eben," she says, stopping me, "it might as well be a world away. And anyway, you belong here."

I don't say anything, but I feel as if I belong wherever she is.

"You can't pull a stick two ways and expect it not to break," she says.

I follow her eyes to the silver creek water.

"I can't take you with me," she says. "I might break you."

I chuckle at that, even though I know it comes out sounding a little sad.

"But what about you? What if you belong here, too?"

She tilts her head back and looks up into the dark sky. "Well, I'm a bird, right? I'll just fly back someday."

Her eyes find mine, and I squeeze her closer to me.

"My beautiful bird," I say, resting my head on hers.

A Bird on a Windowsill

"My beautiful bird."

Chapter Sixteen

Salem
(Seventeen Years Old)

Day 4,577

I know one of these days I'll wake up, and I'll think about seeing Vannah, and she'll be gone. It's happened once already. And I know little pieces of her, like the colors in her eyes or how her head feels on my chest, will slowly start to fade over time. But at least I have her voice.

"Eben."

My thoughts disappear, and I turn toward her. We're at the only park in town. I walked over to the paper from the lumberyard an hour ago to see if she wanted to eat lunch with me. Thankfully, she did.

"There's a quote here," she says.

"What?"

We're sitting on the confession bench—the bench that holds all the town's secrets. In fact, you could probably learn a lot about this place just from this bench alone—if you took the time to decipher it all. Every inch of its surface is covered in light-colored carvings—carvings that say things like: *Sorry, A; Your turn. –C; It was 4 you;* and *RIP JCP, I miss your words.*

I look to the place on the bench her finger is pointing and listen as she reads.

"'There are three deaths,'" she says. "'The first is when the body ceases to function. The second is when the body is consigned to the grave. The third is that moment, sometime in the future, when your name is spoken for the last time.' And there's a name. David Eagleman."

She takes out something from her cloth bag that looks like a camera, but then again, not quite.

"What's that?"

"What?" she asks.

"That," I say, pointing to it. "Is that a camera?"

She looks down at the black and white contraption.

"Yeah, it's a Polaroid. I found it in Uncle Lester's attic."

I don't think I've ever seen one of those in person. I watch as she puts it to her eye, points it at the inscription and then presses a button.

At once, a piece of paper slides out of the camera. She takes it, waves it in the air a few seconds and then holds it out in front of her.

"Hmm."

"What?" I ask.

She slumps her shoulders a little and frowns.

"I don't know. It's sad, I guess. Don't you think it's sad?"

I look at the inscription carved in the wood of the old park bench.

I shrug. "I'm just impressed that whoever took the time to carve that all in there also took the time to put the guy's name there, too."

She gives me a sarcastic look. But I know she's trying not to smile. "But it's sad to think that someday no one will ever say my name again."

"I guess," I say.

She sighs and pushes her lips to one side. At the same time, I put my arm around her and pull her close.

"Someday, there will be no Savannah Elise Catesby," she says. "And someday, no one will ever even remember I was here."

I squeeze her shoulder and smile.

"Vannah, the good news is we won't even be here to know when that time comes."

Her narrow shoulders slump even more.

"I know, but it's still sad."

I kiss her forehead. I think she's so wrapped up in the quote that she doesn't even notice how out of character the kiss is. It just felt right, though, I guess.

"I'll remember you," I say. "I know I won't always be able to say your name, but for the rest of this life and even into the next one, I'll remember you."

She tilts her head back and rests her eyes in mine.

"You promise?"

"I promise," I say.

Her eyes return to the wood and the carved words.

"Maybe you could just come back as a ghost and whisper my name in crowded rooms."

I nod once. "That's exactly what I'll do. I'll be your

name-whispering ghost."

    "Promise?" she asks.

    "I promise."

Chapter Seventeen

Salem
(Seventeen Years Old)

Day 4,584

"Why are we here?" she asks, taking out her camera.

That Polaroid has come with us everywhere we've been since that first day she found it.

"You'll see," I say.

I stop at the top of the levee and look down at the fields below. We're in the bottoms—the floodplain along the river where the soil is the most fertile and all the crops are grown. There are no houses. No trees. No people. Just soybeans and blue sky.

I hear a click and then the machine-sounding slide

of the camera spitting out the photo. And I watch as Vannah takes the picture and waves it back and forth.

"Why are you always taking pictures?"

"They're memories, Eben. I'm taking memories."

She smiles and takes one of me.

"I wasn't even looking."

The sound of her sweet laughter fills my ears. "It doesn't matter."

She retrieves the photo and flaps it in the air.

"You still looked good. See."

She holds it out, an arm's length, in front of us. And I chuckle a little. It's just a picture of the side of my face. But if she likes it, I like it, too, I guess.

"Now, why are we here?" she asks, stuffing the photos and the camera back into her bag.

"Okay," I say. "You ready?"

I can tell she tries not to laugh. "I guess. I sure don't know what I'm ready for, but I'm ready."

"Good." I take a deep breath, and I shout her name at the top of my lungs. "Savannah Elise Catesby."

Vannah jumps a little at my voice, but stays quiet. In fact, everything is quiet for at least a heartbeat or two, until we hear it—her name bouncing off the dirt walls of this place and echoing back at us.

"There," I say, proudly. "Now, your name will always be spoken. For the rest of time, it'll just keep bouncing back and forth in this place forever."

She looks at me. There's a certain kind of usual wonder in her stare, but this time, there's also a kind of awe. And I watch as the whites around her eyes start to turn red.

And then, just like that, she throws her arms around my neck and squeezes me tight.

"Thank you," she whispers into my chest, her

voice muffled.

She holds me like that for a long time, and I hold her back. And in that time, it feels as if heaven itself just opens up on me and sends down everything good from it. And right there, I know that I'd go to the ends of this earth for this girl. I love her that much. And I don't know if it's just years in the making—one day on top of another of just being with her, through her laughter and her pain—or if it's just because we get along so damn well. I can't even tell you why I love her so much. Hell, I can't even tell you what I'm supposed to do with it. Am I just supposed to let her go, let her live her own life? Am I supposed to make her stay? Am I supposed to go with her? Do I ever get to make love to this girl or is holding her hand the best I can ever hope for? I don't know. I don't know the answers to any of this. And I'm not so sure she knows, either. All I do know is that I love her...and that, no matter which scenario is the one that ends up playing out, I'll always love her.

She pulls away from me, halting my thoughts. And then she reaches for my hand. And we stand there, her head resting against my arm, looking at those fields of soybeans as if they're the most beautiful sight in the world.

And then, all of a sudden, she breathes in deeply and then cups both of her hands to her mouth.

"Salem Auguste Ebenezer."

I smile, and together, we wait for my name to come back to us. And sure enough, in the space of two heartbeats, it does.

Salem Auguste Ebenezer.

"We'll always be here, at least," she says, smiling at those green fields. "We'll always be here...together."

Chapter Eighteen

Salem
(Seventeen Years Old)

Day 4,592

"**I**'m going to miss you when I'm gone," Vannah says.

We're at the end of my dock, lying side by side, our backs against the boards. It's one of those nights my grandma would call soft—the kind where the air is warm, the sky is mostly black and the crickets are drowned out by the gentle, cool breeze—warning of a change to come.

Vannah pulls out her camera and takes a picture of the sky.

Meanwhile, my thoughts go back to her. I'm going

to miss her, too. I'm going to miss the way her soft skin feels against mine. I'm going to miss the way her voice wanders with her mind, flowing in and out of dark and light places—sometimes breathy and sometimes cold and thoughtful. But I think I'm going to miss that way she makes me feel the most. Whenever I'm around her, I feel as though the sun's shining down on me—only me. She kind of makes me feel weightless. And I know I'll miss these things because I've already lost her once. And I can't even imagine how much losing her for the second time is going to hurt. But I'll lose her if it means I'll get a chance to find her someday again, because finding her was living the best kind of dream.

She holds out the photo.

"It's just black," I say.

"It's just...here," she says, looking deep into the photo. There's a certain, far-off longing in her eyes.

She keeps her stare on the black image a few seconds longer, and then she sets the camera down—but keeps the photo—and lays her head on my chest. I want to kiss her, but in the back of my mind, that *boyfriend* word lifts its ugly head. So, I just lie there, with our hearts touching. And after a few moments, I can't tell if I feel my own heart beating...or I feel hers. But I just keep lying there, breathing in, breathing out, until the moon is high above us.

"Vannah?"

I lift my head so that I can see her. Her eyes are closed. Strands of her hair are falling over her face and onto my chest. She looks peaceful. It's a sharp contrast to the dark-clouded storm brewing above us.

"Hmm?"

"Are you sleeping?" I ask.

"Mm hmm."

"But you just answered me."

"Mm hmm."

I smile and let my head rest back on the wooden boards of the dock again.

"My heart's awake," she mumbles, just loud enough that I can hear it.

I lift my head, rest my eyes on her face and just watch her.

"My heart's awake, daydreaming of you," she adds.

I pause, my head suspended in the air, my thoughts suspended in time. And then, I smile. I smile and lay my head back down. I don't know if she really is sleeping or if she knows what she just said, but it doesn't matter.

"I love you, Vannah," I whisper.

I can hear leaves in the catalpas around us swooshing, their branches bending back and forth in the wind. I can hear the weather shifting. But mostly, I just hear my heart beating.

"I love you, too."

It's just a soft whisper, but I hear it, loud and clear. I close my eyes and let her words get swept up in the hot and cool air swirling around us. They tickle my skin and then fly up and brush past the willows' arms, swaying to and fro. They'll soon be lost, but I'll remember them. And I'll remember this moment. And mostly, I'll remember her...always.

Chapter Nineteen

Savannah
(Seventeen Years Old)

Day 4,605

It's my last night in Allandale. Tomorrow, I'll leave for the summer and go back to the place I call *home* now. And the truth is, I don't know how to feel about that. I've gotten used to the salty air and the sand and the smell of sweetgrass everywhere. But I'm still not sure if it's quite *home* yet. And truthfully, I miss Aaron when I'm here. But when I'm there, I miss Eben. It's as if my heart's always in two different places.

Eben and I are at Hogan's slab. I love this place. I love the way the water sounds coming out of the concrete—hurried and free. I love the way it always smells like dirt and sycamore trees. And I love that moon—that moon that hangs just in the right place, so that it can light up a path all the way from its spot in outer space to us, sitting here on this little piece of earth.

Eben's been especially quiet tonight. I know he's thinking about me leaving.

I look into his sandy-colored eyes, and he smiles.

I tell myself that we are too good of friends to be in love. But I'm not even sure I believe it. There's a part of me that feels as if I'd leave it all behind for him—if he asked me to. I'd stay here and live with my uncle. I'd finish high school, and I'd go to college somewhere close. And then, I'd work with my uncle. I think we'd make a pretty good team. But then, I know Eben would never ask me to stay. He'd never ask me to leave everything—my family, my new friends, my new life, Aaron.

All of a sudden, I feel his arm around me. He pulls me into his chest, and the familiar scent of his cologne fills my senses. I close my eyes and try to hold onto it.

"The day you stop looking back is the first day of the rest of your life," I whisper near his ear. The saying is carved into the railing on a weathered boardwalk in Murrells Inlet. I saw it one day, and I never thought about it again, until now. In fact, I never really found it fitting, until now. And in the end, I think I say it more to comfort myself than to comfort him.

Several seconds beat on into the wind.

"Turns out, looking back is all I have," he says, in a breathy voice.

His words hit me hard—like a heavy downpour to the chest. I breathe in deeply and breathe out a weighted smile that he can't see.

I love you, too, Salem.

"I'm gonna write you a letter," he says.

"Okay."

It's all I say, and then he nods and squeezes me tighter.

And he did.

One week after I got back to South Carolina, I got a letter. It was from him in his own chicken-scratch handwriting.

He told me he thinks he's getting close to finding my star tower and that if he found it, I'd have to come home right away and dance with him and all the stars. He said he'd take care of Rusty. He said he wouldn't forget me. He said I'd always be his bird.

It was sweet. It made me laugh. It made me cry.

And as I set the letter down onto my desk in my bedroom, my heart hurt. And I was mad at the world. I was mad at my parents for making me leave Allandale. I was mad at Eben for not telling me that he liked me under those stairs in junior high. I was mad knowing that it probably wouldn't have mattered, even if he had. And most of all, I was mad at the fates for making us friends.

It wasn't fair—that I got to know Salem Ebenezer, only to have to leave him behind.

And I remember sliding that letter, along with every Polaroid I ever took that summer, into my favorite book, and I told myself that *he* would forget...that he would forget me and move on—and that would be better for him. It would be better for him

113

to love someone he could touch.

And *I* would forget, too. I wiped my eyes, and I told myself that I would forget every one of those white-bordered memories. And I told myself that I would forget that I ever loved him—that eventually, I would forget the way he bit the inside of his cheek when he thought, that I would forget his beautiful, thoughtful eyes. And mostly, I told myself that I would forget Salem Ebenezer because I feared if I didn't, I would lose myself.

And I went on with my life. I went on living in our new little house in Mount Pleasant—just a bike ride from the ocean. I went on playing volleyball and going to the beach with my new friends every weekend we got a chance. And I went on loving Aaron Anson, so much so, that I followed him to college that very next year.

And I never wrote Eben back.

And as it turns out, that was the last time I heard from him. But that wasn't the last time I ever thought about him. Because after it was all said and done, I guess I had learned one of the hardest lessons that life has to give: *Sometimes, forgetting someone you love isn't so easy.*

Chapter Twenty

Savannah
(23 Years Old)

Day 6,570

*M*y *dearest Savannah,*

   I know by now you've taken over this ramshackle place. I just knew deep down somewhere that you would inherit this little mess of a world someday. I knew even at eight years old that you were destined to have ink under your nails and a writer's pad in your back pocket. You just fit so well here. So, I also knew you'd be the only one to appreciate this place—with its old, stale paper smell and all—when it came time for me to pass it on.
   I'm sorry I didn't spend more time with you or your

sister. I had this place, which by now you probably can imagine has a way of tying ya down. And I knew you had your life. And you're still young and living it; I didn't want to interfere with that. But I do wish now that I had confiscated more of your time. Hindsight's 20/20, I guess.

But anyway, let me get to some things you might need to know. First, there's a safe buried in the corner of this office.

I stop reading, lower the letter and look around. Three corners are stacked as high as I am tall with newspapers. And the fourth has an old blue polyester recliner sitting in it. If there's a safe, he's right about the *buried* part.

I lift the page and start reading again.

And there's a key to it, but I lost that a while back. I'm more than certain, however, that you'll find that, too, if your heart's in the right place.

I smile and furrow my brow at his words but then keep reading.

Paper goes to press Tuesday night. You'll always find a story up at the Casey's. Old Weston Hartfield comes in on Mondays. You'll just have to work through his meanderings. He sets up shop in Ol' Blue, and he camps out there for at least a couple hours. But don't worry, he's harmless. And he knows EVERYTHING. I don't know how, but he does.

And for everything else, there's Jan.

Well, anyway, that's that—about all you need to know. I guess you'll know what to do with the rest. This paper's been my life. Take care of her. She might be old, but she holds all the town's secrets, and that means she'll always be worth something—at least to me...and now, to you, too.

And don't stop living! Like I said, this place has a way of tying ya down. Don't let it!

Love,
Your Uncle Les

I finish and carefully set the letter onto his—my— desk. And I let go of a lungful of air. I can feel my eyes burning as I desperately try to hold back tears—tears that have been a long time coming. I squeeze my eyes shut until I can't feel the burning anymore. Then, slowly, I open them back up and catch sight of a blurry Rolodex. I blink the remaining tears away and move my hand toward it.

I flip through a few of its little white cards, and I notice each one is handwritten. There's a first name and four numbers below the name. And for the first time in a while, I laugh. I flip through some more—all first names, all followed by four digits. I'm guessing these were written before cell phones. And it's clear, they weren't written for anyone who doesn't know the people of this town by their first names.

My eyes leave the Rolodex and move to the old rotary phone on the desk next to it. My mind goes back to my uncle sitting right here in this chair, talking and smiling, that black receiver to his ear, his feet propped up on his desk.

Next to the phone is a big, white coffee mug that reads *Wyandot County's Best Newspaper* in black letters painted down its center. I feel my grin widen, just as I hear that little bell above the door in the front of the tiny building clanging back and forth. It's rigged up to the doorframe by a ruler and baler twine—always has been.

I pick up the letter, fold it and slide it into the top drawer before making my way out of the office. And when I look up next, my breath catches in my chest.

"Eben."

"Savannah?" It's a question, I think. But then again, it's not.

I make my way to the door and throw my arms around him. It takes him a second, but he eventually puts his arms around me, too, and we hold each other for several, long heartbeats.

He smells good. He's still wearing the same cologne he used to wear in high school, and something about that makes my heart happy.

I pull away from him, and his eyes quickly roam over me. And I'm not too ashamed to admit that I like that they do.

"Wow, I, uhhh...," he begins. "Sorry, I wasn't expectin'... I just expected..." He stops and takes a breath. "Hell," he says, with a little grin playing on his face, "I don't know what I was expecting, but I, sure as hell, wasn't expecting you."

I fall back on my heels and feel a comfortable smile pushing its way to my face.

"Salem Ebenezer." I just look at him, taking him all in.

He exhales. "Savannah Catesby."

I do notice he doesn't call me *Vannah*. It's weird, but it has been...

"Has it really been six years?"

He seems to think about it for a second, and then he nods. "It has."

"Well." I bow my head before meeting his same beautiful light eyes again. "You look...great."

Immediately, a bashful air takes over his face, and

if I'm not mistaken, I think his cheeks get a little red, too.

"So do you," he says.

It's definitely Eben—a grown-up Eben, but Eben, all the same.

"You're here."

I nod. "I'm here."

"Since when?"

"Since today," I say.

He slowly bobs his head, as if he's still just taking it all in, too.

"Well, what brings you back?"

"Um," I mumble, and immediately my eyes fall to the old, faded brown carpet. I start to shrug as I look around the little room. "He left it to me."

"Oh." He quickly drops his gaze. "I'm sorry. Yeah. Of course."

"Yeah," I breathe out. I really don't know what else to say.

"He was too young," he says, under his breath.

I nod. "Yeah, he was."

He looks up at me, and our eyes meet. "So, are you here for good then or...?"

I suck in another big breath and then rest my hand on the back of an old desk chair. "I'm here for now, at least."

The truth is I hadn't really thought too much about it. I found out that Uncle Les left the paper to me only a few weeks ago. In that time, I quit my job, packed up my life. And now, I'm here.

I watch him bob his head a couple more times, as if my answer is the one he expected.

"Well, uh, it's good to finally see you again." His words sound sincere. And I don't know why, but that seems to comfort me a little, as if leaving my job and home and my family and friends might have been okay, as long as I got to hear Salem Ebenezer say those words. But at the same time, he also seems distant—not like the Eben I left here years ago.

"Yeah," I agree, gripping the chair tighter. "It's good to see you, too." I wonder if he knows how much I mean that.

It's quiet again. And I'm trying to figure out why it feels so strange to be in the same room with him. Maybe it's because it's been so long. Maybe it's because of the way we left it. Or maybe it's because of the way *I* left it.

"Uh, did you...?" I start to ask. I point to the piece of paper in his hand. I didn't know what else to do with the silence.

"Uh, yeah," he says, shaking his head, as if he's shaking something off. "I did actually come here for a reason. I don't usually wander aimlessly into buildings." He smiles effortlessly. "I have a classified."

I nod, and my smile naturally widens. I'm not sure how much I can handle today, but I'm pretty sure I can handle a classified—and just maybe one from Salem Ebenezer, as well.

"All right," I say, looking around the front desk for a form. I shuffle through some papers and come out with last week's board of aldermen meeting minutes and a stack of printed cartoons. "Uh, here." I turn over the minutes and slide the page toward him. "You can just write down your contact info and information about the item on this. I'm sorry. I don't know where any forms are."

"Oh, it's fine." He takes the paper and grabs a pen from behind his ear.

His action pulls me back. In fact, I might not have ever thought again about him and his habit of keeping a pen or a pencil behind his ear, if it weren't for today. And that thought kind of makes me sad.

He starts jotting down some words, and I tear my stare away from the side of his head and focus on his face while he's not looking. His jawline is squarer than the last time I saw him, I think. And he's got facial hair—a dark five-o'clock shadow. But his eyes are the same dusty shade of brown.

"It's been a good eight years," he says, looking up.

I quickly force my eyes to the counter again. "What?"

"My old Chevy." He haphazardly points in the direction of the parking lot outside. "I'm finally selling her."

"Oh," I say. I look out the window and notice his old truck, and immediately, I smile. We have a lot of memories in that old thing—a lot of memories I haven't thought about in a long time. And I know it's crazy, but for a second, my heart hurts at the thought of someone else driving around with our memories.

"Eight years? That truck was nearly new to you last time I saw you. Has it really been that long already?"

He stops writing, and his eyes find mine. "It's been a while, Savannah."

His words sound sad, maybe even a little angry, but I'm probably just imagining things.

I look down at his left hand, and I notice he's not wearing a ring. I close my eyes and slowly let go of a breath. Him being married would definitely have meant too much time had past. And honestly, I don't know if I would have been able to handle that much.

When I open my eyes again, he's looking at me.

I panic slightly and clear my throat. "You said you'd never sell it."

"You remember that?" He seems genuinely surprised.

"Yeah, I do."

He lets go of a low chuckle. "Good memory." I watch his hand as it taps the surface of the desk once. "Yeah, well, there was a time I didn't think I'd ever sell it. But I guess there just comes a day when you've just got to move on."

He looks at me with an even expression, as if he wholeheartedly meant for his statement to have a double meaning.

I clear my throat again and try to busy myself by shuffling around some of the papers on the desk. "Well then, I guess we'll try to get it sold for ya." I look back up at him and force a smile.

At the same time, he glances down at the sheet of paper and then sticks the pen back behind his ear. "Well, I think that's it." He slides the information my way, along the desk's surface.

I give it a quick once-over, noticing his phone number is still the same.

"How much do I owe ya?"

"Oh," I say, shaking my head. "It's on us."

"Naw." He pulls out his wallet.

"No, really, it's fine," I say, resting my hand on the hand holding his wallet.

I notice his jaw tighten at my touch, and I quickly take back my hand.

"Um." I try my best to recover. "Even if I wanted to, I wouldn't know what to charge you right now anyway."

He narrows his eyes at me. "You sure?"

"Yeah. Positive."

"Well, thanks." He stuffs his wallet back into the back pocket of his faded blue jeans.

"It's nothing," I say.

He steps back but doesn't bother turning. "It's good that you're back."

I smile without even realizing I'm doing it. I've been trying to tell myself that all morning. But it sounds so much better coming from his lips, for some reason.

"In fact, you've probably forgotten how fun this little town can be," he adds.

I laugh an honest laugh. "Maybe."

He turns and makes his way to the door.

"Eben," I say, regaining his attention.

He slowly turns back toward me.

"We should catch up."

His eyes meet mine. It's only one, momentary look, but it's so very cryptic. I can't tell if that's a *yes*, a *no* or a *hell no*.

I'm a little sad that he doesn't seem as excited to spend time with me as I am to spend time with him.

But eventually, he nods and gives me a small smile. "And thanks again," he says, tipping the bill of his cap, right before he slips outside.

The little baler-twine bell sings, alerting me he's gone. And I breathe out a long, unsteady breath.

"Salem Ebenezer," I whisper to myself. *It's been a long time.*

My eyes fall to the page on which he scribbled the classified: *1968 Chevrolet C-10 1/2-ton pickup with custom trim. Original 327 V8 with 3-on-the-tree transmission. A little rust in the rockers, but great body. Runs well. 200,000 miles.*

His name and number follow. I hear the truck start

up outside, and I see the sun's glare from its windshield bouncing off the big front window. I don't know how he has the heart to sell that old truck.

I know I don't.

I glance at the piece of paper one more time, and then I fold it in half. And then I fold it in half again, and I stick it into the back pocket of my jeans.

Chapter Twenty-One

Savannah
(23 Years Old)

Day 6,573

I hear the bell ring above the door. I'm in the back corner office going over everything with Jan—Jan, the secretary, the graphic designer, the ad specialist, and right about now, my everything.

"I'll get it," Jan says, starting to stand.

I'm sure tending to everyone who walked in the door was her job, too—up until today.

"No. I'll take care of it. We need a paper out this week."

Jan smiles and sits back down, and I make my way to the door.

"Hi," I say, before I can even see the figure standing behind the front desk.

"Hey."

I immediately recognize the voice.

"You know, we should really stop meeting like this," I say, as he comes into view.

He laughs and dips his head. His laugh is just how I remember it—low, even and authentic.

"I was just dropping by the ad I had been working on with Jan," he says. "I added a couple things, and..."

"Is that you, Salem?"

He peers back into the other room, as Jan's voice echoes through the narrow hallway.

"Yeah, it's me. I brought the ad back."

"Thanks, dear," Jan says. "You can leave it with Savannah. We'll get it in next week."

"All right. Thanks," he says to Jan. And then, just like that, his attention is back on me.

"Well, how's all the sortin' through everything coming?"

"It's coming," I say, trying not to sound or look as frazzled as I feel.

He rolls up the piece of paper and then unrolls it.

"Is it for the lumberyard?" I ask.

"Hmm?"

I eye the page in his hand. "The ad."

"Oh." He glances down. "Yeah."

He sets the piece of paper onto the desk, but it stays rolled up. I watch as he tries desperately to straighten it.

"It's fine," I say. "I'm sure we can read it all the same."

He lets go of the ad, and it curls up into a tube again.

"Do you work there now?" I ask, even though it seems pretty obvious with the *Ebenezer Lumber* sewn in orange thread onto the pocket of his navy shirt.

He nods. "Yeah. I actually went to school for business. I do most of the buying these days." He shifts his weight to his other leg. "You know, Dad's tryin' to make that early retirement, and as soon as I know my way around all the movin' parts, I'm pretty sure the only place we'll see him is fishin' on the lake...or on some golf course somewhere." He pauses to laugh under his breath.

"Golf? I didn't know your dad played golf."

"He took it up a couple years back." He looks up at me now. "He's awful, but he loves it."

I lower my eyes, and at the same time, try to conceal my smile. "Well, that's all that matters, I guess."

"Yeah," he says. "His golfing buddies would beg to differ."

I laugh, and this time, I don't even try to hide it. But all too quickly, there's a silence that fills the space between us. My first instinct is to fill it, but I don't have the slightest idea of what to fill it with.

"Well, I should probably get goin'," he says, patting the surface of the standing desk. "I only snuck out to drop that off."

"Yeah," I say. "Of course."

"I guess I'll be seeing ya around then."

I nod my head once. "I guess you will."

"And you're right, we should catch up."

"Yeah," I agree.

He smiles and then turns and slips through the heavy, wooden door, cuing the baler-twine bell.

When he's gone, I take the rolled-up page and go back to Jan.

She's staring at me as soon as I make it through the doorway to the little corner office.

"What?" I ask.

"You two have history?"

I drop my gaze and try my darnedest not to grin. "You could call it that."

"I'd call it more than that, but that's just me."

"What?" I try not to look surprised.

"Oh, don't think I didn't hear the words you two were sayin' in those long pauses out there."

I start to laugh. "I almost forgot how this town worked."

"What do you mean?" Jan feigns hurt.

"Really," I say, "the only thing I'm concerned about right now is getting a paper out this week. ...And maybe getting a new phone for the office. The last place I saw a rotary phone was in an antique store in Asheville."

Jan smiles, takes the ad, pushes up her glasses and goes back to her computer. "Then, a paper you will have, Miss Catesby."

I let go of a thankful breath.

"But you might want to have a conversation with that boy...sooner than later," she adds.

I give Jan a questioning look.

"I don't even want to know what that means."

"Okay, but don't say I didn't warn you."

I keep a curious eye on Jan. But I'm not worried. I know Eben. In fact, there's not anyone in this town that knows him better than I do.

Chapter Twenty-Two

Savannah
(23 Years Old)

Day 6,575

I sit down onto the couch and bring my knees up to my chest. I'm tired. I'm tired from moving. I'm tired from trying to get this place organized. I'm tired from trying to get caught up with everything at the paper.

I rest my head back on the couch and close my eyes. And just when I do, I hear a loud bang come from the kitchen.

I quickly lift my head, as adrenaline sprints through my body.

I'm trying to place the sound, when it comes to me.

It's water—gushing water.

I jump up and run to the kitchen. It looks normal. Nothing's out of place. But I still hear the water. It's coming from under the sink.

I throw open the cabinet.

"Shit."

Bending down, I close my eyes and reach for the valve that shuts the water off. As I do it, cold water sprays into my face.

"Shit, that's cold," I gasp.

I get the valve turned off, and the water stops, but my face and my sweatshirt feel as if I've just run through a sprinkler.

I stand and wipe my eyes with a dry part of my sleeve.

I want to cry, but I laugh instead.

Of course. Of course this would happen tonight.

I grab a towel from a drawer and start soaking up the water from the floor of the cabinet. And when I get most of it up, I drop the wet towel into the sink and think for a second.

I remember the guy who always fixed our plumbing when we lived back here. I think he's retired. But he had a son, who I went to high school with, and I think he was going into the business. I wonder if he's still here.

Salem's the first person I think of that would know that. I go back into the living room and grab my phone.

It feels kind of weird sending him a text, but then again, it also feels pretty normal, too.

Savannah: Hey
Salem: Hey
Savannah: Is it too late?
Salem: No. What's up?

Savannah: I'm sorry to bother you, but a pipe just busted under my kitchen sink. Does Jason still do plumbing?

Savannah: Salem?

Salem: I'll come over.

Savannah: No, it's okay. You don't have to. I turned off the water. I'll survive until tomorrow.

Salem: You're at Lester's, right?

Savannah: Right

Salem: Give me ten minutes.

Savannah: Seriously, you don't have to come.

Salem: I'm on my way.

Savannah: Okay. Thank you. ☺

"Hey." I step back to let Salem in. "You know you didn't have to come. I..."

I stop because his eyes are lingering on my sweatshirt.

I look down and notice it might as well be soaked. But before I can say anything about it, he smiles and steps past me.

"Looks like you got into a fight with a fire hose," he says, over his shoulder.

I laugh to myself and close the door.

"Water was going everywhere." I follow him into the kitchen. "Luckily, I was here."

"Luckily," he says, kneeling down at the sink.

I notice he has a small arsenal of tools in his hands.

"Looks like you've got a broken slip-joint nut."

I kneel down next to him and peer under the sink, too.

131

"A broken nut, huh?" I laugh under my breath, mostly because I have no idea what he's talking about.

"Yeah, not a big deal." He crawls under the sink, so that only his bottom half is sticking out. "I'll just replace it real quick."

"And that will fix it?" I try not to stare too long at the place his shirt has come up around his abs.

He's been working out.

"Yeah, should."

His words make me jump. But I quickly realize he can't see me. His eyes are still glued to the piping. So, I relax again and continue to examine him— from his toned stomach all the way to his scuffed work boots.

But after a minute, he's pawing at the floor. I see the wrench, and I figure he must be aiming for it, so I pick it up and put it in his hand.

Our hands touch briefly, and he stops. And for only the second time tonight, he lifts his head and looks at me.

"Thanks," he says, with a warm smile.

"You're welcome."

The feel of his hand sends a warm shock through my body, starting at my fingertips. And it's only a tiny moment, but it brings back so many memories of my hand in his.

I watch him as he goes back to pulling and replacing little metal parts. I do have to admit there's something attractive about watching him work.

"That should do it."

He reemerges from under the sink, and it forces my thoughts to a halt.

"You're done already?"

"Yeah, it was a pretty easy fix."

I softly clear my throat, trying not to give away that

I was just thinking about how attractive he looked.

"Well, thanks. I really appreciate it."

He stands and turns on the water in the sink. This time, it comes out from the faucet and not the pipes underneath.

"Not a problem."

He brushes his hands on the pant legs of his jeans and starts gathering up his tools.

"Well, do you want to stay a little while? We could catch up. I have..." I stand and go to the fridge. "I have Gatorade...and cheese," I say, looking inside my empty refrigerator. "And now, thanks to you, I have water." I gesture toward my sink with a big smile plastered to my face.

He grins and lowers his head. "No, I need to get going."

"Oh, okay." I can't help but feel as if he's brushing me off. But then again, he did come over to fix my sink—not to have a reunion.

He moves toward the door, and I have no choice but to follow him.

"By the way, how did you know I was here, at Lester's?"

His eyes quickly cast down to the floor at our feet. And he shrugs. "It's a small town. Can't hide your business, remember?"

He looks back up at me and smiles.

"Right," I say, nodding.

Then he turns to leave.

"Thanks again...for coming out. I know it's late. ...I owe you."

"No, it's fine," he says, turning back only for a second. "You don't owe me anything."

I smile, and he pushes through the screen door.

"Have a good night, E."

"You, too."

I watch him get into his truck. And a flash of his headlights later, he's gone.

I step back from the door and gently close it. I'm relieved the pipe is fixed. I wasn't excited about not having water in the kitchen for the rest of the night or about having to deal with getting it fixed tomorrow, for that matter. And it was sweet of him to come over. He didn't have to. I didn't even know he could fix a broken sink.

But something also has me feeling a little unsettled. Something about him tonight was different. He was short—polite but to the point.

I fall back against the door and let it catch my weight.

What if Eben has changed? What if we've both changed? What if we just can't be the same two people we used to be?

A heavy feeling fills my chest, making it hard to breathe. I think it's a gentle reminder of how much time has passed—a forewarning, of sorts, of the wall that's grown up between us.

My only hope is that we can break it down again.

Chapter Twenty-Three

Savannah
(23 Years Old)

Day 6,576

"You look all professional with that camera."

I feel an elbow to my side, and I turn and look up. It's Eben.

"Oh, hey," I say.

For the first time since I've been back here, I'm surrounded by the people of this town again. Young, old, it seems as if they're all here—dancing, drinking, talking.

"You retire that old Polaroid?"

I laugh and glance at my camera. "No, I've still got it. It's just Polaroids don't print so well in newspapers."

He tilts his head back and smiles. "Aah, I see."

I watch him force his hands into his jeans pockets and rest back on his heels. He seems like his old self. He seems...happy.

"How's the pipe holding up?"

"What?"

"The sink."

"Oh, yeah. It's great. Thank you again."

"No," he says, shaking his head. "It was my pleasure."

I smile. "I didn't know you were a plumber, too."

"Miss Catesby, I fear you've been gone too long. There's probably a lot you don't know about me."

His last words cross into a new light. They sound darker—almost foreboding, in a way.

"So, how was the rest of high school and the East Coast and the last...what is it...half a decade of your life?" he asks, changing the subject.

I take a second. I can't help but notice that, *tonight*, he seems to be in a talking mood. It makes me feel a little lighter, somehow.

"It was good," I say.

He gnaws on the inside of his cheek and nods once. "I heard you were a big shot and won some award at a paper down there recently."

"Wow, word sure does travel fast in these parts," I say, in my best Southern drawl.

He looks at me curiously—as if he doesn't know what to think of my accent.

"Like tongues of fire lickin' up straw," he confirms.

I think he tries to say it in a Southern accent, too, but I'm pretty sure whatever accent that was, it doesn't exist in real life.

I let go of a heartfelt laugh. It feels good to laugh with him again.

"Plus, your uncle liked to brag on you," he adds.

My smile quickly fades. I miss Uncle Les—the times we shared and those we didn't.

"It must be kind of hard steppin' back into this small-town stuff, though," he goes on, breaking me out of my thoughts.

I look at him and notice his dusty eyes first. They're darker tonight, as they focus on something across the room.

"Mount Pleasant isn't that much bigger," I say.

"Ha." He laughs. "The Walmart in Washington employs more people than live in this town."

A laugh instantly catches in my throat.

"So, how'd you get the honor of inheriting *The Town Herald* anyway?"

I shrug. "I was the only one who knew anything about the newspaper business. I'm happy to have it."

I see an old woman dancing with a boy. I only vaguely recognize them, but not enough to remember their names. I snap a photo. I never wrote about foreign affairs or high-profile criminal cases out east, but I did cover imports and exports and the shipping news, which is the news that won me the award. But dancing grandmas... There aren't too many awards for dancing grandmas.

I push back my shoulders and continue to scan the faces.

The bottom line is that I have a paper to revamp and get settled before I can even contemplate going back to that world again. And who knows? Maybe there will be something here worth staying for.

I catch Eben staring across the room again, but this time, I see a girl. And something that feels an awful lot like jealousy washes over me.

"Who is she?"

His eyes dart to mine. "Who's who?"

"The girl in the corner—the one you keep trading glances with."

He smiles and takes a breath. "Can't get anything past you."

"Were you trying to? Get it past me?"

He narrows his eyes at me and only grins.

"That is," he starts to say but then stops when he catches her eye, "Anna, my girlfriend."

I don't say anything for a second. I only look at the girl with the long, dark hair in the corner and then quickly refocus my attention on him.

"You have a girlfriend?"

He nods. "I do."

My gaze falls to the floor near my shoes. I think I'm just trying to sort it out. And even when I feel his eyes on me, I still don't look up.

"Savannah?"

"Yeah, I just...um, you never had a girlfriend."

My stare lifts to the pretty girl in the corner of the room. She's talking to another girl now.

"I had a couple girlfriends in college, actually."

"Really?" My eyes go to him.

I don't know why I never thought to think Salem Ebenezer would have a girlfriend. He's attractive—tall, muscular, sweet. Of course he would have had a girlfriend...or two.

"So, you met her in college?"

"No," he says, shaking his head. "I met her here. She moved here after school."

I suck in a quick breath, and at the same time, I stuff a pad of paper into my camera bag.

"When did you want to catch up?"

"What?" I ask.

"You said you wanted to catch up."

"Oh, yeah." I feel distracted, all of a sudden. "It can wait, I guess."

"I tell you what, how about I come by the paper sometime."

"The paper?"

"Yeah. If I see your car out front, I'll stop by, and if you're not too busy, we can catch up."

He's looking at me when he finishes. "Yeah, okay," I mumble. "Sure."

Suddenly, I don't know how to feel.

"Um." I clear my throat and busy myself by easing my camera back into its bag. "Well, I've got to take off."

"Okay," he says, nodding. "I'll see you around then."

I force a smile, and with that, I turn. And I leave. I leave the crowded, outdated dance hall and the pretty girl in the corner...and the boy, who once upon a time, used to be mine.

Chapter Twenty-Four

Savannah
(23 Years Old)

Day 6,577

"You must be Weston Hartfield," I say, as the old man with a crooked cane walks, unannounced, into my office.

I watch as he carefully falls into the blue recliner, just as if he's done it a million times before. And I wouldn't be surprised if he had.

"Sure as the day is long," he says, in a soft but rough voice.

I nod. "Well, it's nice to finally meet you. I heard you might stop by."

"Yeah, as long as I'm kickin', I'll be here. Every

Monday."

I type another sentence out on a story I'm working on—just so I don't forget it. And then I look up.

He seems comfortable in the chair now. His cane is propped up against the blue polyester. An old seed dealer cap is resting on his knee.

"Nothin' too much to speak of this week," he says. "All's pretty quiet this time of year."

I nod and smile.

"Hey," he says, as if he's just thought of it, "you doin' business with that Ebenezer boy?"

I'm a little thrown off by his question, until I notice him eyeing the lumberyard ad sitting on my desk.

"You ought to be careful with that boy."

I examine the old man, as he stares back at me with a raised brow. What's left of his hair is white. He's got a beard. It's white, too. He'd probably make a pretty good Santa Claus.

"That's funny," I say. "You're actually not the first person to tell me something like that."

"Yeah, well. That should tell you somethin'."

He goes to resituating himself in the old chair.

"Why is that? Why is everyone warning me about him? I've known Salem since we were young."

"Well, he's changed since he was just a boy," he says. "Well, he's got that girlfriend. And she seems like a good girl—a little too fancy for my liking, but a good girl, I guess. But that Salem, he's changed."

"How so?" I try not to sound too curious.

"Well, you know, he's been working real hard on something mysterious. And ain't nobody knows what he's doing."

"Something mysterious?"

"Yeah," he confirms with a head nod. "You know,

he's probably working for the government or something. That's the only thing I can think of."

He stops and shakes his head, and then he seems to get lost somewhere outside the window behind my desk for just a moment.

"He could be doing some kind of testin' or, uh..." He pauses, as if in thought. "It could be he's making some kind of weapon or something. You know, for the, uh..."

He looks at me, and I just stare blankly back at him.

"The, uh, you know?" he goes on.

"The government?"

"Yeah," he says. He tugs on his beard and then points a finger at me. "Or it could just be drugs, you know. All these kids these days. They start off good kids, and then they just get caught up in the drugs, you know?"

"Drugs?" I say, trying to keep my smile to myself.

"Yeah, bad stuff." He shakes his head. "Real bad stuff. You don't want to get involved in those drugs."

"Okay," I say. "No drugs."

He seems satisfied with that comment.

"So, where is it that he's doing all this mysterious stuff?"

"Well, most likely it's just one of those things," he clarifies. "I don't think he'd be doing all three."

He holds his stare on me, so I nod.

"Right, just one. Testing, weapon or the drugs."

"Right," he repeats. "But that's the problem. No one knows which one it is. He's got barricades all set up at the bottom of Sheppard's Hill."

"Sheppard's Hill? Outside of town?"

"Yeah," he confirms, "that's it. And you can't see

anything from the road. Believe me, I've tried. You can't even see anything from the air. That's what I hear, anyway. I didn't look myself, of course. I don't got no helicopter, and I don't got one of those fancy computers where you can see everything from the sky."

I nod, in thought, as the room grows quiet.

"You know, maybe he's just building a house," I say, after a moment of the silence.

"Yeah, that's exactly what we thought, at first." He puts his finger to his lips. "So, we asked him. And then he got all secretive about it. Never did get an answer out of the boy. And not too long ago, Keith Sumter saw big, unmarked flatbed trucks going up the hill." He shakes his head and furrows his brow. "Real fishy stuff."

"Okay," I say. "And you said he's acting weird."

"Oh yeah. I know he's an Ebenezer. I know he was raised right. Those Ebenezers are good people, you know?"

"Yes, I know," I confirm.

"It's just, you know, all that went on right before he went off to school... And then lately..." He stops and starts over. "He's just around, you know? ...But he's not around."

He looks at me with one eye squinted shut and his head cocked to one side. I think he assumes I know what that means.

"What do you mean 'not around'?"

"You know, not around," he says. "These days, he's either at the lumberyard or he's up on Sheppard's Hill. You don't see him anywhere else. Just one of those two places. That's it."

"Testing or making a weapon...or drugs?"

He slowly nods his head. "Now, you're gettin' it."

"So, what all went on before he left for school?"

His eyes quickly find mine.

"You know." He flails his hand in the air. "When the devil got to him."

I keep my stare in his, but I don't say anything. I'm waiting for him to elaborate, but he never does. And after a few moments of us just staring at each other, I look down at my keyboard and then push out a long, steady breath.

"Okay, Mr. Hartfield, I've got a lot of work I need to finish up. I appreciate your information, but I'm sure those boys up at Casey's are missing you by now."

He smiles. "Yeah, I reckon you just might be right about that."

Slowly, he starts to get up. It takes him a little while to climb out of the chair, but once he does, he balances himself with his cane and stands up tall. Then he shoves his cap back on his head.

"It's good talkin' to ya."

I nod. "I'll see you next Monday, I suppose?"

"If I'm still kickin'." He smiles over his shoulder. "And you can call me Weston."

I smile, too. "Okay."

He's almost out of my office, when he turns back around. "You know, you're sure a hell of a lot prettier than Ol' Les."

I bow my head and laugh to myself.

"That's good to know."

He nods once and then turns and walks out the door.

When he's gone, I sit back and let my head rest against the back of the chair while my eyes get stuck on the white ceiling above me.

I'm pretty certain everything Hartfield said today

was bullshit. But even bullshit has a little truth to it. Eben's doing something up on Sheppard's Hill. I just wonder what it is.

Chapter Twenty-Five

Savannah
(23 Years Old)

Day 6,581

I pass a sign that reads Sheppard's Hill Road and drive about four hundred meters, when I stop. There's a fairly new graveled path leading off the county road, and it's been barricaded off with big, metal gates.

This must be it.

I pull off to the side of the road as much as possible, put my car in park and get out.

The path behind the barricades goes up into the woods. I try to follow it with my eyes, but like old Weston said, I can't see anything through the trees. And even if there were no trees, it's very likely that I couldn't see anything from the county road anyway. The gravel looks as if it goes back a pretty long way. And there's a cedar post and barbed wire fence that looks as if it runs around the entire property.

I step back and catch sight of a sign on one of the metal barricades. It reads: *No trespassing. Violators will be prosecuted.*

I push my lips to one side. It's a normal *no trespassing* sign, but it does seem a little extreme, especially since people around here usually just use purple spray paint to ward off trespassers.

I look back up the graveled path and rest back on my heels.

"What are you up to, Salem Ebenezer?"

"The girl in the peacock dress."

The voice startles me, but then I immediately recognize it and turn around.

I'm back at the office now, attempting to work on some stories for next week.

"What did you say?"

"You've never heard that one?"

I look down at my dress and at the green and gold feathers that are pressed into the fabric. Then I narrow my eyes at Salem, start to smile and then shake my head.

"The girl in the peacock dress," he recites. "She chose the world with no one in it. And now, with a brand new pair of wings, she sails the seven seas at night, just as she always wanted. Free. Untouchable, but free."

I love his gentle voice. It's comforting. But as he says his last word, I feel my smile start to fade.

"Still writing poems, I see?"

He shakes his head. "Nope, that's an oldie but goodie."

I feel my grin coming back. "Well, I don't know what to think of your poem."

He lifts his shoulders and then lets them fall. "Think of it as the soulful words of a lovestruck teenager. Nothin' more," he adds.

"Lovestruck?"

He laughs and then shakes it off.

"Okay," I say, not pushing him—even though I'd love nothing more than to push him on that one.

I go to filing some of my notes into my desk organizer.

"I saw your car outside. Thought I'd stop by."

"All right," I say.

He finds the recliner in the corner of the office and falls into it. I stop what I'm doing and watch him as he makes himself comfortable.

"You're quite the talk of the town, you know?"

Instantly, he stills and finds my gaze.

"Me?"

"Mm hmm. Turns out you're a secret spy for the government."

He looks genuinely amused. "Wow, that one I haven't heard."

I smile wider but keep my eyes on him.

"What are you doing up there?"

"What? Up where?"

"Sheppard's Hill."

He drops his stare and exhales loudly.

"Nothing," he says, taking off his cap and running

his fingers through his curls. "It's nothing. And I can assure you, I'm not working for any government."

I laugh and shake my head. "I never said you were."

My eyes find his and stay in them for a little while before I go back to filing again. I'm a little off-kilter with him in the room. I don't know how to act around a Salem who has a girlfriend.

"Do you miss it?"

I look back up.

"South Carolina," he clarifies.

I focus on that old rotary phone for a minute. I still haven't replaced it.

"I miss my family. And I miss the ocean sometimes," I admit, taking a seat in my office chair. "And I miss that you can go there—to the ocean—and no matter what kind of day you're having, that salty air just takes everything away—until all you're left with is yourself and God."

I pause and smile as my eye catches on a yellow bird sitting on a branch right outside my window. "And I miss the swimsuits hanging over the shower and the beach towels strewn across the porch railing. And I miss the sand—that awful sand that never goes away. I miss that, too."

I glance back at Eben, and then I gather some notes on my desk before shrugging my shoulders. "But this place is in my blood. So, I guess you could say that me and Allandale get along just fine, too."

He nods, almost as if in agreement. But my mind stays on his question. I hadn't really thought about missing Mount Pleasant, until now.

"But it's funny," I say, catching sight of that yellow bird outside again. "Even when I was gone from here, I still always dreamed of this place. In almost every dream, Allandale was the setting."

His eyes narrow just a little.

"Is that weird?"

"Depends," he says.

I cock my head to the side.

"Are there white hogs chasing you with animal balloons that look like frogs?"

I laugh. "No."

"I had that dream once."

"Really?"

"Yeah. What do you suppose that means?"

"That you're weird."

"Yeah," he says, smiling, "you're probably right."

I pick up my coffee mug and take a sip.

"You know," he says, "they say you dream most about the places you wish you had a little more time in."

"Do they?"

He nods.

"I think it goes for people, too," he says.

My eyes find his.

"They say you dream most about the people you wish you had a little bit more time with, too."

I'm quiet, as I take a breath. "Do they, now?"

He nods and then drops his gaze. "That's what they say, anyway."

"Hmm," I hum.

I set the coffee mug back down onto the desk and listen as the room grows silent.

"Well, I'm on my lunch break," he says, breaking the purr of nothingness. "Thought it'd be a good time to catch up. You busy?"

I take a deep breath in and then look around the room. There are boxes and papers everywhere. But I guess they're not going anywhere.

"Sure. All right."

I watch him make himself more comfortable by propping his ankle on his opposite knee and resting his elbow on the arm of the chair.

Meanwhile, I sit back in my own chair.

"First off, maybe you can tell me why there's an old recliner in my newspaper office."

The chair is faded blue and worn, but it's still padded, and it looks somewhat comfortable, although I've never felt the urge to see for myself.

"Oh," he says, looking down at the arm of the chair he's sitting in, "this old thing?"

I just smile and nod.

"It's the sittin' chair."

"Aah." I make sure not to look too satisfied with his answer.

"Well, it's mostly for Old Weston Hartfield," he says. "In fact, I think he brought it here himself and planted it right here in Lester's office one day. He got tired of sitting in that old, wooden desk chair that used to be here, I guess." His eyes move to a chair, filled with papers, in the opposite corner of the room.

I bite my bottom lip and simply nod. "Aah, that makes sense."

"Yeah," he says, "he's usually got the latest gossip—who got their pickup stuck on Keiser Hill Road, who made the most outlandish comment around the coffee table in Casey's on Sunday morning..."

"Who's into drugs on Sheppard's Hill," I add.

Eben stops and locks eyes with me.

"I'm doing drugs now, too?"

I shrug. "Apparently."

"Unbelievable," he says, starting to smile.

He's quiet then, as if he's thinking. Then all of a sudden, he sits back even further in the chair. "So, tell me about high school."

I give him a look to let him know that I know he's changing the subject. And then I shrug. "Like I said, it was good. I mean, it was high school—the same old, rectangular cafeteria pizza for lunch, volleyball, weekends at the beach, prom, graduation. Nothing I'd like to relive necessarily. But still good."

"Weekends at the beach," he recites, in a low voice, smiling as he says it.

I catch his devilish stare, and I already know what he's thinking.

"Yeah," I say, "and on holidays, we traveled to private islands and partied all night on big, expensive yachts."

"What? Really?"

I laugh. "No."

His smile widens. "Okay, you got me. But you have to admit that *weekends at the beach* sounds a little more glamorous than *weekends at the slab*."

I think about it. "I just might prefer the slab."

"What? I'm thinking that East Coast sun might have crossed some wires in your head."

I lower my gaze and laugh to myself.

"Well, what about you?" I ask, looking up again. "I see you became that basketball star."

"You saw that?"

"Yeah, the papers from your senior year are archived in the back. I might have taken a peek at them."

He chuckles. "We won state."

"I saw that. Congrats."

He looks at me and gives me a bashful smile. "Well,

Laura Miller

I figured that was probably as bright as my star was gonna shine in that department, so I just focused on school after that."

I nod. "So where did you go? For school?"

"Missouri."

"Oh. Good business school, I hear."

He bobs his head once. "Pretty good."

"And you?"

"South Carolina," I say. "Uncle Lester tried to get me to come here to Missouri, too. But I guess, when you're eighteen, the best journalism school in the country doesn't hold a candle to a boyfriend."

"Yeah," he says, shaking his head. "I couldn't leave mine either."

I look at him with narrowed eyes. "You had a girlfriend in high school, too? After I left?"

"No. Dillon. Hell, he might as well have been my girlfriend. He followed me to school and then whined every weekend for me to spend more time with him."

A wide smile takes over my face. "What does Dillon do now?"

"He works out in St. Louis, at a bank."

"Aah. You miss him?"

The sound of his laughter fills the little room. "Only on those lonely nights."

I laugh, too. And even if I'm not supposed to, I can't help but think how much I like this moment—how much I like to hear him laugh.

"Whatever happened to the high school boyfriend?" he asks, after our laughter fades. "That one you met down there?"

"Oh," I start to say, shaking my head, "we broke up a semester into college."

"So, he's the one you followed there?"

153

"Yep, that would be him."

"So, who'd you leave behind to come here then?"

"Me?" I ask, and immediately, I just know it comes out sounding awkward.

Salem just nods. "Yeah, you."

"No." I shake my head. "I dated in college, but... I worked a lot," I finally settle on. "So, no. No boyfriend."

"Hmm," he hums.

"What?"

"Nothing."

"No, what?"

"It's just hard to believe, I guess," he says, and then stops.

"What's hard to believe?"

"I don't know." He sits up in the recliner. "That you don't have a boyfriend. It seemed as if you always had a boyfriend."

I just shrug.

"I expected you to be snatched up," he says. "I mean, I think I just half-expected you'd be engaged or even married by now."

"You would probably know if I were engaged or married."

"No," he says, "I probably wouldn't."

I find his eyes and stay in them for a few heartbeats. There's something hidden in his wayward look, and I can't, for the life of me, figure out what it is.

"Hell," he says, dropping his gaze, "you might have a line outside this door here tomorrow, if you're not careful."

I fake a laugh.

"You think I'm kidding?" he asks.

I look at him and his goofy grin for a second

without saying a word.

"You haven't changed much, Salem Ebenezer."

"Apparently, that's not the talk of the town."

"No," I agree, "apparently not."

His eyes burn into mine, as if he wants to say more, but he never does, and the moments fall away.

"Well," he says, looking at his watch, "I better get going. It was nice catching up with you, Miss Catesby."

He stands, and I just smile. "Yeah," I say, "it was."

He walks to my office door, but before he leaves, he turns and tips his cap.

"We should catch up more later."

"All right," I say, without even thinking twice about it.

And then, he's gone.

Chapter Twenty-Six

Salem
(23 Years Old)

Day 6,586

"Savannah Catesby."

I hear Dillon call out her name, and I look up.

"It's about time you stopped by," he says.

She smiles and walks over to Dillon. Dillon stands and gives her a hug, being careful not to spill the drinks in her hands.

"And you know this guy, of course," Dillon says, resting his hand on my shoulder.

Savannah nods and smiles. "We've met a couple times."

I smile at her. And then, if I'm not completely

crazy, I think there's a look that lasts a little too long. And I think Dillon notices it, too.

"Well," Savannah says, "we're across the room." She gestures toward a table of girls from high school on the other side of the bar. "But I'm going to drop these drinks off over there and come right back for a second."

"Sounds good," Dillon says.

She smiles at him, glances at me and then walks away from our table.

I take a drink from my bottle, actively trying to avoid eye contact with Dillon. I know he's looking at me.

"Where's Anna tonight?"

"Working," I say.

He's quiet, and when I look up, he's just slowly nodding.

"How much time have you been putting in at that paper over there?"

"What?"

He gives me an accusing look.

"What are you talking about? I was only there once—to catch up."

"I'm not saying," he says, putting up his hands in surrender. "I'm just saying."

"Dillon." I shake my head.

"Come on, Salem. I know you liked her. Everyone knows you liked her. You've been chasin' after that girl since kindergarten. What's different now?"

"What's different?"

"Yeah," he says.

"What's different, if you haven't noticed, is that I'm seeing Anna—and I've been seeing Anna for a while now. What's different is that I haven't seen

Savannah in six years. What's different is that when Savannah and I knew each other, we were both just kids."

I finish, and he's staring at me with a set of narrowed eyes. I try not to look directly at him.

"Does she know what you're doing on Sheppard's Hill?"

My eyes instantly go to his. He already knows the answer to that.

"What about Anna then? Does she know what you're doing on Sheppard's Hill?"

"Dillon, I'm not in the mood for this."

"What are you two talking about?" Savannah comes over and takes a seat next to me.

Dillon looks at her and just smiles one of his cool, confident smiles—the ones he does best.

"You," he says.

She laughs. "Then why do you both look so serious?"

She elbows me, and I force a smile.

"Your girlfriend here?" she asks.

"No, she's working." The words come out shorter than I intended them to.

"Okay," she says.

I can tell she looks at me, but by the time I look up, she's already trading questioning glances with Dillon.

"Is everything okay?" she asks.

"It's fine," Dillon says, leaning back in his chair. "It's all fine."

"Okay, well... I heard you were in St. Louis," she says to Dillon.

"Yeah," he says.

"You like it?"

"Yeah, it's not too bad."

"Tracy said you still get back quite a bit."

"Tracy's here?" Dillon's eyes light up.

"Yeah." A big smile takes over Savannah's face. "You better get over there if you want to talk to her."

He laughs and looks across the bar. "No, it's fine. I don't want to mess up your girl party. I'll just talk to her later."

"Okay, well, you guys be safe tonight. I'm going to get back over to them."

She rests her hand on my shoulder after she stands. And then she's gone.

Dillon rubs the back of his neck, sits back in his chair and then just stares at me.

"What?" I ask.

"Nothing."

I clear my throat and take another drink.

"Look, man," he says, "I don't know what's going on exactly, but I do think you should know that Jake Buckler has been eyeing her all night."

"Where is he?" I ask, looking behind me, trying my best to maneuver as covertly as possible.

"Over there," he says, glancing at a place on the opposite side of the little bar.

I find him, and sure enough, after only a few moments of watching him, I notice he takes a long look in Savannah's direction.

"What in the hell is he doing?" I ask.

"It looks, to me, as if he's moving in on your girl."

My face turns stern and quickly finds Dillon. "She's not my girl."

I get up, polish off the last of my bottle and set it down hard.

"I'll see you later, Dillon."

"What? You're leaving?"

"Yeah."

That's all I say. And I turn and make my way out of the bar. And when I get outside, I suck in a long, deep breath.

I probably should have just stayed home tonight.

Chapter Twenty-Seven

Savannah
(23 Years Old)

Day 6,590

I walk into my office and immediately go to the calendar on the wall.

"Do you miss him?"

I freeze, my back to him.

"How are you always in here?" I ask, turning to see Salem sitting in the old recliner.

He shrugs. "I'm mostly a face. They don't notice if I'm gone too much."

I smile. "Why didn't I hear the bell?"

"Well, I would suspect that it's because your music is too loud." He points to his ear. And immediately, I remember the earbuds in my own ears.

"Oh," I say, pulling at the wires and realizing, at the same time, that I'm shouting. "That's probably a good point."

I set the earbuds onto my desk.

"Well, do you miss him? Your uncle?"

"Yeah," I say, my eyes getting stuck on the old wood surface of the desk. My initials are carved into the corner. I remember doing it one day, not too long after I learned how to write them. But instead of getting mad, Uncle Les picked up the little screwdriver and carved his initials right under mine. I run my fingers over the *L* and the *K*.

Thinking of Uncle Les still turns up mixed emotions. I've had time to accept it, but I'm still sad. I barely saw him the last six years of his life, before the cancer took him away. I remember everything about spending that last summer I had with him. My mom must have known, even then. And I remember those long days I'd spend here growing up, too. The musty paper smell, his stacks of notes on his desk, the endless sticky notes stuck everywhere, this two-room office— all of it felt like home, in a way. Hell, he's probably the reason why I got into newspapers in the first place.

"There's a lot of people here that miss him," he says.

I sigh, pick up a paper and stuff it with a weekly ad. "That's nice to hear."

He nods. "It's true."

"So, what else did I miss?" I ask, trying to change the subject before my eyes go to tearing up on me.

He looks at me as if I'm crazy.

"Here?"

"Yeah," I say, "with you. I mean, clearly, I missed

162

the whole part where you got a girlfriend."

He just smiles. "Don't look so surprised, Vannah."

My breath catches in my throat, and I feel my own smile start to fade.

"What?" he asks, after a few seconds, as if he doesn't know why I lost my grin.

"Nothing. I just... You called me *Vannah*. I just haven't heard you call me that in a long time."

"Oh." His eyes are wide. "I don't even know where it came from."

"No, it's fine," I quickly say. "It's nice."

I can tell he's at a loss for words.

"Well...?" I ask again.

He gives me a blank stare, and it makes me laugh. "You and...?"

"Oh. Anna?"

"Yeah," I confirm.

"Oh." He sits up in the chair. "She's great, really. We met at one of Dillon's parties in St. Louis about six months ago."

"Hmm," I hum. "So, are you guys like...really serious then?"

"Oh, one sec," he says, reaching into his buzzing pocket.

"I'm sorry," he mouths.

I shake off his apology to let him know it's fine, as he pulls out his phone and puts it to his ear.

"Yeah," he says. "No, I can pick it up."

I stuff another ad into a paper.

"Sure," he says, after a brief pause. "I love you, too."

I stop what I'm doing and look up at Salem. He's busy stuffing his phone back into his jeans pocket. He has no idea that my heart just took a beating with those four, little words of his.

"I'm sorry. Now, what did you say again?"

I force myself to take a breath. "Oh, it was nothing."

He looks as if he doesn't quite believe me. "Okay, then."

I watch as he shifts in his chair. "Can I ask you somethin'?"

I nod. "Sure."

"Did you read my letter?"

I drag in a long breath. I think I knew this was coming. I expected it, eventually. And of course, I know exactly what letter he's talking about.

"Yes."

"And...?"

I open my mouth, but nothing comes out, so I try again. "Salem, that was a long time ago."

"As a friend," he interjects. "Just a friend asking a friend."

His look is gentle and almost pleading.

"I'm sorry I never wrote back," I say, slowly setting the paper down. "I'm sorry I never texted or called. I'm sorry I..."

I stop. He's piercing me with his light brown eyes, as if my answer's not good enough. And I know it's not.

"I didn't know what to do," I confess.

"We were friends," he says. "You could have just written back. I mean, at the very least, we were friends, right?"

"Yeah. We were. We are," I say.

I look at him. He's biting the inside of his cheek and nodding his head.

"It wasn't anything you said...or didn't say," I add.

"I'm just...sorry. I really didn't know what to do. I was a teenager. I had a boyfriend. And you were here. And I was there. And I felt as if I were in two places. And I didn't feel as if I was being fair to Aaron...or you. So, I just did what I thought was right, I guess."

He's still slowly bobbing his head when I finish. And then he stills.

"One more thing."

"Okay," I say, but secretly I'm scared to hear it.

"You did like me, right? I mean, you said you... I mean, I didn't just make that up?"

He's wearing this face that looks as if he'll just break in half if I don't answer his question the right way.

"I did," I assure him. "Yes, of course." I barely get the words out.

"Were you in love with me?"

I freeze and fix my eyes on him.

"Yeah." I don't even think about it before I say it. "I did love you. I still love you. ...You're my oldest friend," I add, being careful not to cross any lines with him and his girlfriend.

He softly chuckles and then drops his gaze.

"What?"

"I asked you if you were *in love*," he says.

I don't know what to say after that, so I just go back to stuffing the last ad into the paper and setting the paper onto the pile. I don't know what he wants me to say. He's the one with the girlfriend. He's the one who just told her he loved her. He's the one...

"Wait," I say, "why did you want to know?"

Seconds draw out, and I can hear that clock on the wall and its unforgiving ticks.

"No reason," he eventually replies. "I guess I just

always wanted to know that, and now...I do, so..."

"Wait." My mind is just now starting to process his question. "Were you in love? Like really, in love..."

Before I can even get the rest of the sentence out, he stops me.

"Did you read the letter?"

I nod.

He keeps his eyes on me, but he doesn't say another word. And after a few more moments, he gets up.

"I'm meeting Anna in Washington in a half hour. I should probably get going."

"Yeah, okay." I cross my arms against my chest.

"Okay," he says. And then he tips his old baseball cap and escapes through the door.

And then he's gone.

And I'm just left with a thought: *Salem was in love...with me. And I broke his heart. And it still matters to him.* But then, it's quickly replaced with another thought: *But he just left to go see Anna—whom he loves.*

Chapter Twenty-Eight

Savannah
(23 Years Old)

Day 6,593

I'm rooting through an old box I stuffed full of ticket stubs for movies I don't even remember seeing anymore and old Valentine's Day cards from boys I'd much sooner forget, when I find it.

I push the box away with my foot and bring the letter closer.

Vannah,

I haven't stopped looking for your star tower. I know every day I'm getting closer. I can feel it.

Rusty's doing good. He does cat things all day. He stares at me while I'm sleeping and while I'm eating and while I'm watching TV. In fact, he pretty much just stares at me all the time. The usual.

Your name is still echoing off the levees down in the bottoms. I went there and listened for it the other day, and sure enough, there it was. Savannah Elise Catesby—loud and clear.

I wish you didn't have to leave again. I wish I could have gone with you. And I know you have a boyfriend. But I still just wanted you to know this:

One day I met a little girl when I was just a boy. And we spent our days on sawdust piles and teeter-totters. And cherry Popsicles melted into paper airplanes and then late-night movies and then things with wheels. And those days turned into years. And one by one, those sawdust piles dried up. And those old, wooden teeter-totters turned into boat docks and concrete slabs and truck cabs under dark skies and starry nights. But still, that same little girl remained.

And somewhere in all that sawdust and concrete, that little girl stole my heart, and I was too busy being in love to even know it.

I'm going to miss you, Vannah. But more so, I'm going to miss us. Because us *is a pretty cool thing. And I hope someday you see that, too. Until then, my bird, I'll just be waiting.*

Love,
Eben

I finish and reread one line: *I was too busy being in love to even know it.*

My heart sinks. *How did I not see that?*

I'm letting the old words soak in when I notice a stack of Polaroids. I set the letter down and pick them up.

"Our memories," I whisper, under my breath.

I shuffle through the photos, stopping to remember the moment I took each one. And with each one, I know my smile is growing wider.

"Savannah."

My heart almost leaps right out of my chest.

I look up to see Salem standing in the open doorway to my house—Lester's old house. It's a nice day; I was just letting the place air out a bit.

I quickly stuff the letter back into the box. "Salem?"

"I saw your car out front," he says.

"Oh." I haphazardly try to capture the stray pieces of my hair and stick them back into my ponytail.

"You wanna get some lunch?"

My eyes fall to my sweatpants and old tee shirt.

"You look great."

I start to laugh. "I don't. ...But I'll go."

He waits, as I stand up, still holding the photos.

"What do you got there?"

I stop and follow his gaze to my hand.

"Oh, it's nothing." I shake my head and hide the Polaroids under a book on the table. "Just let me get my keys."

"Sure thing," he says, rocking back on his heels.

"This is weird."

"What's weird?" I ask.

"You and me. You and me, sitting down, talking about our days over cheeseburgers."

I smile. "Well, technically, they're just burgers."

Tiny wrinkles form at the corners of his eyes.
"Who runs out of cheese?"

I shrug. "Diners run by friends of Dillon Denhammer run out of cheese."

He lowers his head and laughs to himself.

"But anyway, I don't think it's that weird—you and me eating some lunch, that is." I take a bite of my burger.

"Savannah, I never thought I was gonna see you again."

I stop chewing and look up. There was something in his voice—some frail, vulnerable piece—that made me take notice.

"Why would you think that?" I ask, after I swallow.

He shrugs. "Because I had no reason to believe I would."

His sharp thought stabs right into my heart and stays there. When I made the decision not to write back to him, I don't think I ever intended never to see him again. I think I just...didn't think at all. I think I just made a choice that I knew would get us through the next few days, and maybe the next few months.

"And then one day," he goes on, "there you were, in that newspaper office, just standing there, staring back at me."

I fight back a small smile.

He stays in my eyes for a few, fleeting moments, and then I panic and grab a fry. "How's Anna?"

Something in his look shifts, and he clears his throat and stares down at his plate. "She's good. She just got a promotion."

"Oh, really? What did she get promoted to?"

"Oh, it's another step up in her certification. She

does hair at Kerlin's Salon."

I smile. "That's great."

"She's really excited," he adds, as I take another bite of my burger.

"Whatever happened with you and Andy?"

"Who?"

"The high school boyfriend."

"Aaron?" I ask.

"Yeah, maybe it was that."

I laugh on the inside.

"Turns out he was cheating on me."

"Oh," he says, looking sorry now that he had ever brought it up. "I'm sorry."

"No, don't be. I didn't lose too much sleep over it."

"Really?"

"Well, I didn't. But he might have. Turns out, my friends snuck into his dorm room in the middle of the afternoon and took everything he owned, including his mattress, and threw it out the window and right onto Hudson Hall's lawn."

I pick up my drink and take a sip from its straw.

"I had crazy friends," I add.

We both laugh. We laugh as if we never missed out on all those years. We laugh as if we're still those same, two junior high kids, hiding out under those stairs. But eventually, it grows quiet again. And I'm okay with the quiet, too. I'm okay with just me and him and my thoughts.

I just can't believe that same boy I knew when I was five is sitting across from me now. He even looks different from how I remember him at seventeen. The man in front of me is tall and strong and filled out in all the places you'd expect a good-looking man to be filled out in—even down to the biceps peeking out from his fitted tee shirt sleeves.

"Why do you always wear that key?" I ask.

His eyes find mine fast.

"What key?"

"That key at the end of that chain," I say, pointing a fry at the silver popping out from his collar.

A surprised glow washes over his face.

"Oh, come on, Eben."

Instantly, he cocks his head. "You called me *Eben*."

"Yeah?"

"You haven't called me that since the first day you got back here."

"Hmm." I try to think back. "Really?"

"Yeah."

I push my lips to one side. That's probably about the time I found out he had a girlfriend. "Anyway, about the key."

I watch the edges of his mouth slowly turn up.

"That's the key I gave you, isn't it?"

He just stares at me, as if he doesn't know what to say.

"How did you know?"

"I always knew," I say.

His eyes narrow, right before he pulls on the chain. And sure enough, a shiny, little key pops out of his collar.

"You haven't found it already, have you? And you're keeping it all a secret for yourself?"

He laughs. "You would know if I just so happened to stumble upon an observatory that belongs to this key."

This time, *I'm* the one with the narrowed eyes. "Would I?"

He lowers his gaze and smiles.

I want to know why he kept it. And I want to know why he still keeps it around his neck. But I don't intrude. Not today, anyway.

"You're gonna find me that star tower," I say, biting into another fry. "And then, the first thing you're going to do is find me."

His lips curve up even more, and then he nods. "Of course. Of course, I will."

And then carefully, in almost a calculated kind of way, his eyes find mine.

There are sounds from the café—plates clanging, silverware dropping, people murmuring—but they're all being drowned out by the silence between our stares.

You don't have to say it, Salem.

I know.

We both know our trip down memory lane is over. It was over long before it ever started. It was over the day I left town six years ago. It was over once I spread my wings and flew back to my temporary home.

Chapter Twenty-Nine

Savannah
(23 Years Old)

Day 6,601

"**S**avannah, right?"

I look up from my paint swatches and notice a man facing me.

"Right," I say.

"I'm Jake Buckler." He holds out his hand, and I shake it.

He's a tall guy—clean-shaven, dark hair, pleasant smile.

"You're running the paper now, aren't you?"

I nod. "I am."

"Well, welcome," he breathes out. "I'm sure you've

heard that already."

"Well, it's more like welcome back, I guess. I grew up..."

"Jake," Salem interrupts, taking a place right next to me.

Jake falls back on his heels and takes a good look at Salem.

"Salem," he says. It's a simple acknowledgement.

"Hey, I heard you were going out of town soon," Salem says.

Jake bobs his head once. "Yeah, for the weekend."

"Well, we should get that lumber order finished up for ya before you leave then. Here, Joey will fix ya right up."

"O-kay," Jake says. There's an obvious hesitation in his voice.

"Joey," Salem calls back to the register.

Within seconds, a sandy-blond-haired kid, about sixteen, bounces up to Salem.

"What do ya need, boss?"

"Jake, here, needs to finish up his order. Can you manage that?"

The boy bobs his head at Jake. "Sure thing. I'll get ya taken care of over here at this register."

The boy faces Jake and points to a corner of the building.

"Okay," Jake says. He turns back toward me. "Well, it was nice finally meeting you, Savannah."

"You, as well," I say.

"Maybe I'll have to stop by the paper sometime and see how much it's changed since I've been there last."

Before I can say anything, Salem jumps in.

"Nothin's changed."

Both Jake's and my gaze instantly go to Salem.

"Still the same old place," Salem says. "All right, Joey will take ya back there." Salem rests his hand on Jake's shoulder and points in the direction of the register.

I notice Jake eye Salem's hand on his shoulder. It's one of those looks that says he knows more than he's letting on. Then he smiles politely and follows the boy. And when they're out of earshot, I look to Salem.

He's robotically fiddling with the top of a paint can. I know he's trying to avoid eye contact with me.

"Salem."

"Hmm?"

"What was that?"

"What was what?"

He stops turning over the one paint can and goes to reading the back of another. But I don't say anything else until he finally looks up at me.

"You know *what*," I say, in a half-scolding tone.

He shrugs. "I don't know what you're talking about."

I give him my best straight face, but then I quickly decide it's probably just easier to let this one go. "Fine. You got my paint swatch thingy, right?"

"What?" He seems distracted.

"The paper thing that has the paint color I need on it?"

"Oh, that. Yeah, I've got that."

"Okay, then, I guess I'll see you later."

"See ya," he mumbles.

I get to my car in the parking lot, throw my bag onto the passenger's seat and slide in behind the wheel.

"Savannah."

I look up to see Salem jogging across the black

asphalt.

I take my hand off my keys in the ignition and sit back in the seat.

"I'm sorry," he mouths, when he gets to me.

I roll down the window.

"For back there," he says. His eyes motion back toward the lumberyard building.

I feel a lopsided smile slowly inching its way across my face. "But why? What were you trying to do? Is he like, a serial killer or something?"

He shrugs and looks down, as if he's trying to avoid my question.

"Salem," I scold.

"No. No, he's not a serial killer...that I know of."

"That you know of?" I try not to laugh.

"I don't know. It's not like I've done a criminal background check on him."

"Salem!"

"What? I just don't like you talking to him."

I stare straight ahead, straight through the windshield, trying to figure out what to say next. I'm more than a little speechless right now.

"Look, I know it was stupid. I'm sorry."

He's quiet after that.

"Is there something wrong with him?"

He keeps his head down.

"Salem, tell me."

"No," he says, shaking his head. "No, there's nothing wrong with him. He's a good guy."

"Then, what on earth?"

He still doesn't look up. "He's a guy."

I pause because I think I don't hear him right, at first. But when he doesn't say anything else, I start to laugh.

"I'm sorry to break it to you like this, Salem, but I talk to guys every day. And I'm still here—healthy and emotionally sound and all."

"That's not what I mean."

Out of habit, I press my lips together and narrow my eyes. "Salem, you're gonna have to help me out a little here. I have no idea..."

"It's because you're mine," he says, looking at the ground again.

Instantly, I feel my brows knitting together.

"You're my friend. My bird," he says, with a smile. "I'm sorry. I'm just... I know you're not mine like that. I know."

I'm scrambling for words. My mouth is open, but nothing is coming out.

"I don't know," he goes on, before I can even think of anything. "Sometimes, I think about other people knowin' you better than I do, and... They can't know you better than I do. I mean, I haven't seen you in a while, I know." His eyes are shadowed by the bill of his cap. "But I know you, Savannah. I know you better than anybody in this town. And sometimes... Sometimes, I feel as if that makes you mine."

I still don't know what to say, but despite myself, something comes.

"I get it."

That's all I say, and he just lowers his head so that I can't see his face anymore behind his baseball cap.

"Do you really?" he asks. "Or are you just sayin' that to make me not feel so crazy?"

I look into his eyes, now unhindered by the cap. "Yeah," I assure him. "I do. I mean, sometimes, I think I feel the same way."

"Really?"

"Yeah. Like, just the other day, you were talking to Anna... And this is going to sound crazy and totally out of line, but..."

"I don't care," he says, cutting me off.

I meet his stare; he's got this little smile playin' on his lips. And it makes me smile, too. "Okay," I go on. "You were talking to Anna at Lakota's, and I wanted to say *hi*, but I felt as if I'd be intruding, so I just kept on walking, until I walked right out the door. And it wasn't until I was outside that I stopped. Right there in the black of night, I stopped, and I thought: *But I had him first*." I let my gaze fall to the steering wheel. "I know that's crazy, but..."

"Then I'm crazy, too," he quickly says.

My eyes find his. His are warm and welcoming, happy and fiery—everything I always loved about them.

"Because I had her first." He keeps his stare in mine.

His words are like spring water to a thirsty desert.

"Do you think we'll always feel that way?" he asks.

I lift my shoulders and then let them fall, and then I slowly shake my head. "I have no idea."

The words come out sounding more weighed down than I had anticipated.

"It feels kind of like I'm in limbo with you here," he breathes out.

I look up at him. My heart starts to pound in my chest. I want him to say he wants me. I want him to say he loves me. Only me. *Not her. Me.* And I want him to say it—if only for the sake of our past.

"But the day you stop looking back," he says.

And with that, my heart breaks in two. It breaks for an *us* that is no more, as moments trudge on in painful silence.

"Is the first day of the rest of your life," I whisper.

He lets go of a small, guarded smile and then taps the roof of my car before taking a step back.

Meanwhile, my attention falls to the steering wheel, and I quickly work to put the pieces of my heart back together, until his words slip back into my thoughts.

"Your bird, huh?" I look up at him and try to smile.

He laughs to himself and lowers his gaze before finding mine again.

"Well, this is my windowsill, so you must be my bird."

"But you forget," I say, smiling thinly. "I have wings."

"Well, then why do you keep coming back if you're not my bird?"

I shrug. "Maybe because I like your windowsill."

"Or maybe it's because you like me."

My brittle grin burns into a thoughtful one. I don't know if he's joking or if he really means it. And worse, I don't know if it's true or not. I love him, but I'd *like* him a whole lot better if he loved me, too.

"That might be a little presumptuous," I say, trying desperately to hide the fact that his last comment means more to me than I think he intended it to.

He tilts his head in my direction and lifts one shoulder before pressing his lips into an easy smile.

"I'll see you later, Eben."

He nods and tips his cap.

"Later, Vannah."

Chapter Thirty

Savannah
(23 Years Old)

The little bell above the door rings just as I'm finishing up a story. I hit *save* and make my way out to the front of the office.

"Hi."

I hear the voice, and I look up to a man with eyes the shade of coffee, smiling back at me.

"Oh, hi. Jake, right?"

"Right," he says, bobbing his head.

For the first time, I notice he wears his hair a little longer than most guys around here. And I watch as he forces his hands into his pants pockets and assesses the little office. "The place looks nice."

I look around. My eye catches on the little old desk in the corner first and then the old clock on the wall and then the same old papers still in their stacks.

"It looks the same," I say.

He laughs.

"Yeah," he says. "It looks the same."

It's quiet for a second—just long enough for his eyes to amble back to mine.

"Are you doing anything Friday night?"

Immediately, I suck in a breath.

"Um." My gaze quickly hits the floor. And my first thought is *Eben*. My second thought is *Anna*. My third thought is Eben saying that Jake is a good guy. And my final thought comes from my Uncle Lester: *Don't let it tie ya down.*

"No, actually," I say, looking back up. "I'm not."

"Can I take you out?"

An instant smile takes over my face. He looks kind of cute the way he's standing there, motionless, in his nice black slacks and white, collared shirt—as if all his hopes are hanging on my answer.

"Yeah. Okay."

It's only now starting to sound as if maybe it's a good idea.

"Good," he says, bobbing his head again. "I'll pick you up at seven, then?"

"All right," I agree.

He nods his head once more. "Okay, well, I guess I'll let you get back to work then." He turns to leave but then freezes before he gets to the door. "Uh, where should I pick you up exactly?"

I feel my lips twisting into a grin. "That would help, wouldn't it?"

"It just might," he agrees.

I laugh softly.

"Do you know where Lester used to live?"

"Yeah, out on Kohl City Road?"

"That's it. I'll be there."

"Good," he says. "Can't wait."

I smile wider, and then he slips through the door.

I haven't got a clue as to what I've just gotten myself into, but I guess it wouldn't be my first mistake, either.

I rub my eyes and then gather my hair into a ponytail. But I can't stop thinking. A part of me is excited—excited to meet someone new, excited to start a new life here. Yet, there's a part of me that still feels stuck—stuck in the past, stuck in someone else's life, stuck in a dream.

I walk back into my office and fall into my chair. And after a few minutes of my mind wandering here and there, I find myself smiling at the wall, thinking about this new stranger—Jake Buckler. He stood there, in this office, just moments ago, with his beautiful smile and his dark eyes and his commanding self, and he bashfully asked me on a date. It was one of the cutest things I've ever witnessed. I would have been crazy to have said *no*. And who knows, just maybe this Jake Buckler can rescue me from the past. ....*Just maybe.*

Chapter Thirty-One

Savannah
(23 Years Old)

"Hi." I open the door to Jake.

"Hi," he says, finding my eyes. He's wearing a big smile, and for a moment, I get lost in it.

"Uh." He shifts his weight to his other leg and drops his stare to his hands. "I wasn't sure if you liked flowers, but I thought of you when I saw these the other day."

He holds out a box the size of a big shoebox.

"I noticed them on your office door...and the wall...and the desk...and the phone... And I'm pretty sure I saw a couple on your steering wheel, too.

Thought you might be running low."

I take the box and laugh. "My uncle always said that sticky notes keep you sane. It's a learned behavior, I guess." I meet his gaze. "This is sweet of you. Thank you. But how'd you find such a big box?"

"I have my ways," he says, grinning. "Hopefully, that'll last you a day or two."

"Maybe." I laugh and then set the box onto the table. "Well, come in. I just have to grab my purse."

I turn and head for the other room.

"You look beautiful."

His words make me stop. It's almost as if he had just discovered something new, and he couldn't wait to tell me.

Slowly, I swivel back around.

"Thank you. You look great, too."

I stand there for a second, in his eyes. There's something about him. There's just something about him that's so different from most people around here. He's kind of Hollywood, in a way, with his slightly longer haircut and his perfectly faded jeans. And I'm not really sure why that even matters, but somehow it does because I'm trying my darnedest not to blush.

But then suddenly, I remember my purse.

"I like your place."

I pause on my way back to him and steal a glance around the room, trying to take in what he's seeing.

It does look nice, I guess. I hadn't really stopped to look at it yet. All of Uncle Lester's papers are gone now. The walls are all freshly painted. My new furniture is mixed with some of Uncle Les's old pieces, like his little writer's desk and his antique hall tree. I couldn't bear to store those in the dusty attic.

"I like the art."

His eyes are caught on the photo in the entryway.

"I don't know if it's art, necessarily," I say, trying not to laugh. "It's Sullivan's Island in South Carolina. And it's really for just when I miss the ocean."

He looks into the photo a little bit longer, as if he's examining every detail, every shade of blue. And then his attention is back on me.

"It's beautiful."

I lower my eyes, trying not to look awkward. "Thank you."

"Did you take it?"

"I did."

"You've got an eye."

I laugh under my breath, as his eyes linger in mine. I feel as if I should say something to fill the silence, but oddly, I don't mind existing in his stillness, really. There's something strangely appealing about being the subject of his interest.

"Well, are you ready, Miss Catesby?"

My face beams, as if it's a mirror image of his. And I nod. That's all I do. I'm afraid if I try to speak, nothing will come out of my mouth.

I follow him out of the door and to his car in the driveway. He has a nice, shiny, black sports car. Immediately, I feel bad that by the end of the night, it'll be a nice, dust-covered, sandy-colored sports car, thanks to the gravel road.

"So, did I hear you right? You're from here?"

"Born and raised. You?"

"Uh, no," he says, opening the door for me. "I'm from a little town in Illinois. Chester. Home of Popeye."

I laugh. "*That*, I didn't know."

"What? The Chester part or the Popeye part?"

186

I smile. "Both."

Who knew? Such a beautiful man—from the Home of Popeye.

"Do you work here?" I ask.

"Yep," he says, after he starts the car. "Well, around here, anyway. I mostly work in Washington. Real estate. Been here for several years now."

I nod.

"Is that where you were...South Carolina?"

"Yeah, my family moved to Mount Pleasant, right next to Charleston, when I was sixteen."

"Aah, so how is it being back?"

I take a moment to think about it.

"You know, nobody's asked me that yet." *I don't even think I've asked myself that.* "But it's different, I guess."

"Different how?"

I look over at him. There's something about a guy driving a stick shift that makes me feel at home. But there's something strangely fascinating about a guy who drives a stick shift to a fast car.

"Well, I think I just expected everyone and everything just to freeze when I left," I say. "But they didn't." I smile to myself. "I think I half-expected it all to look exactly the same when I got back. But in the end, everything just kept moving on and growing up without me, I guess. And I think I just lost my place. And now, I'm just trying to figure out where I fit in again."

He's nodding when I finish.

"But I do love it here," I say.

"I can tell."

He makes a face then, as if a thought gets stuck in his throat.

"What?"

His eyes wander off the road and onto me.

"I hope you don't mind me asking."

"No, go for it. I ask people questions all day. I suppose it's only fair I get asked one every now and then."

"Yeah," he says. "I guess that's fair."

He makes sure to look into my eyes when he smiles next. And I swear, something in me melts a little.

"Is there something going on with you and Salem Ebenezer?"

Without even thinking, I instantly take in a sharp breath and force my attention outside the passenger's window. Tree after tree floats by. I'm not sure what I was expecting his question to be, but I'm pretty sure *that* wasn't even on my radar.

"No," I say.

He nods, as if he's weighing my answer.

"Okay, I just had to ask. He was acting strange the other day. I didn't know."

"No, I know," I say. "We grew up together. That's all."

I notice his wide smile.

"What?" I'm hesitant to ask, but my curiosity is too much for me sometimes.

"Oh, it's nothing," he says. "I just know how that goes."

I turn my focus to the side window again for a split-second. "How what goes?"

"Oh, I just grew up with someone, too. A girl. We spent every waking minute together."

"What happened?"

He clears his throat. "I moved away...for a job, for a change. We gradually lost contact. Last I heard, she was living in Chicago."

I nod, not really knowing what to say.

"Do you miss her?"

He shrugs. "I miss our friendship sometimes, I guess." He finds my eyes. "But no, I don't miss her. I've come to learn that letting your past dictate your future is pretty messy business."

I smile, but I don't really feel it, as my stare gravitates toward my window again. "You're probably right about that one," I agree.

Tree after tree just keeps floating on by. Meanwhile, I'm trying to tell myself his comment *didn't* sound more like a warning.

"Do you like French?"

"Hmm?"

"Food. I guess I should have asked that earlier."

"No, it's fine. I like any food."

"Good," he says. "I think you'll like this place."

Chapter Thirty-Two

Savannah
(23 Years Old)

Day 6,621

"Why the long face?"

Salem's downtrodden expression doesn't change, as he takes a seat in the old recliner.

"Bad day." He says the words and then casts his eyes to the floor.

"O-kay."

I type out another sentence on my computer before I lose my thought. Then I stop and look over at him.

He's sitting there, slumped over, with his head

down.

"You want to talk about it?"

Slowly, his gaze wanders up to mine, and if I'm not mistaken, he smiles.

"I've just got a lot on my mind today. That's all."

"Like...?"

"Like things I should have done, things I shouldn't have done. That kind of stuff."

I sit back in my chair.

"Have you ever watched a train go by?" I ask.

He looks up at me blankly while seconds tick out of that old black and white clock on the wall.

"Yeah, of course," he eventually answers.

"Well, have you heard the way the rails hiss after it's gone?"

He seems to consider it. "Yeah, I think so."

"It's the sound of the wheels hitting the inside of the track," I say.

"Okay," he says, nodding.

"But the thing is," I go on, "the sound is with the train. It's not the tracks themselves. And eventually, the train gets far enough away that you can't hear the hissing sound from the wheels anymore. But my point is that we think the hissing sound is coming from the rails the train leaves behind. But the sound is really coming from the train."

I stop, and he just stares back at me with knitted brows.

"Am I supposed to know what that means?"

His silly laugh makes me smile.

"It means the train's gone, Salem. Quit worrying about it. You're just hearing the sounds of the old things echoing back. But they're not really there. They're gone. They're with the train. And now, all *you* can do is focus on what's right in front of you."

He doesn't say anything. He just starts chewing on the inside of his cheek.

"Does that help?" I ask, hesitantly.

"Yeah, unfortunately, it does." He stops gnawing on his cheek and refits his cap over his head.

I notice my laptop went to sleep somewhere in our conversation, so I close it. And when I look up again, his eyes are on me.

My breaths get short as I get lost in his familiar stare. I can't know what he's talking about. But this whole conversation has me thinking about us—about what we were, about what we could have been, about what we'll never be. It makes my heart ache, knowing that there's a train out there with all our memories on it, and it just keeps moving down that track, getting farther and farther away.

I pause before I say my next words.

"Eben, can I ask you something?"

"Shoot," he says.

"Why did you keep the key?"

A crooked smile finds his face. "You haven't given up on findin' that star tower, have you?"

I hold my stare in his, trying my best to playfully scold him without saying a word.

He drops his gaze and shakes his head. "I don't know. Maybe I wanted to hold onto my childhood. Or maybe," he says, looking back up at me, "I wanted to hold onto you."

I freeze.

"You were the first girl to ever give me a piece of her treasure," he says.

With that, I relax again and feel a small smile returning to my lips.

"I put it on a chain after you left that first time, back when we were in high school. I've worn it ever since."

I nod, refusing to say anything—still just taking it all in.

"Well," he says, hitting both arms of the blue chair with the palms of his hands. "I best be going."

I watch him get up and walk to the door. But then he stops, turns and covers his mouth with his fist.

"How do you get over somebody?"

My eyes ask him the question before my voice ever does.

"What?"

He glances down at the carpet and then quickly peers back up at me from underneath the bill of his cap. "I mean, how do you get over somebody...you love?"

I know I must have a stunned look plastered to my face.

"It's for Dillon."

"Oh." I feel my heart restart again. "But...Tracy *does* actually like him, you know?"

"Really?" He looks genuinely surprised.

"Yeah."

"Huh." His eyes wander up to the ceiling. And then he pauses before he gets his next words out. "But just for shits and grins..."

It takes me a second to realize he still wants an answer. "Oh," I say, dropping my gaze to the surface of my desk. "How do I move on?"

"Yeah, I mean, you've been in relationships before."

I feel my chest inflate with a breath.

"Well, you've been in a couple, too."

"Yeah, but I was never... I just want to know how

you did it." His words come out rushed.

"Okay. Well, I guess..." He meets my stare. "I guess you just keep breathing."

"Breathing?"

"Yeah," I say, "and one day, you notice that you're not breathing for them anymore."

Something in his look—some little, unguarded part—freezes on his face.

"Who are *you* breathin' for, Vannah?"

His eyes are locked on mine, until I drop my gaze to the desk again. And then I shrug.

"Myself, I guess."

He's nodding when I look up. There's a thoughtful look in his eyes, but it's also kind of sad, in a way. Long, silent, tense moments pass between us. I don't know what to say, so I just don't say anything.

"So just keep breathin'?" he asks, eventually.

I think about it for a second and then nod. And then I watch his chest rise and then slowly fall.

"Eben?"

His eyes meet mine.

"You can't love someone well, until you're breathing for yourself first."

He keeps his eyes on me, but I can't read them.

"Thanks, Vannah."

And with that, he slips through the door and into the evening, as the sound of that little bell ricochets through the office.

Chapter Thirty-Three

Savannah
(23 Years Old)

Day 6,635

"I'm coming out of the grocery store with some lunch when I see Eben. And I'm about to call out his name, but then I stop. There's someone else with him.

It's Anna.

I don't move. I don't call for him. Instead, I watch them. I don't even think I mean to; I just do it.

They're laughing. My eyes follow his hand as he pushes her hair back from her face. And then she presses her nose to his and gives him a kiss on the lips. And that's when I look away. And before I know it, my legs are carrying me in the opposite direction.

"Savannah."

I hear my name, and instantly, my eyelids fall over my eyes. *God, if you ever thought about giving me the power of invisibility, this would be a good time.*

Reluctantly, I start to turn. And when I get all the way back around, I see him and Anna walking toward me.

I adjust the paper bag in my arms.

"I'm not sure if you guys have officially met," Salem says, when they reach me.

He looks nervous.

"Anna, this is Savannah."

I hold out my hand.

"Hi," I say.

She takes my hand. "I've heard so much about you."

I'm curious as to what she's heard.

"I've heard a lot about you, too," I say, not really knowing if that's true or not.

There's an awkward pause, and then Anna spins around and faces Salem. "Well, honey, I'm going to be late. I should go. I'll see you later." He squeezes her forearm and gives her a sweet smile.

I shouldn't, but I envy her for that smile and the way he touches her arm.

"It was nice to meet you," Anna says, right before she turns to leave.

"You, too," I say.

My eyes mindlessly follow her, until she disappears behind the building.

"Are you heading back to work?"

I hear him, but I don't think I register the fact that he's directing his question at me.

"Savannah?"

196

"Hmm?" I say, almost as if I'm waking up from a daydream.

"Are you going back to the office?"

"Uh, yeah," I say, nodding once.

"Can I walk you back?"

"No. It's okay."

"But I want to."

I find his eyes, mostly, I think, because I'm a little caught off guard by his eagerness.

"I need some relationship advice," he whispers, covering his mouth with his hand.

I breathe in deeply and instantly breathe out a cautious smile.

"Please," he begs, playfully.

"Okay. Okay, fine."

We start to walk. And he shoves his hands into his pockets and sighs. I look up at him, but he doesn't look at me.

"What is wrong with you?"

"What?" A shocked look blankets his face.

"Why would you think something's wrong with me?"

"Because you're acting weird."

"I'm acting weird?"

I nod, as if it's clearly obvious. "Yeah."

He laughs, takes his hands out of his pockets and grabs the paper grocery bag from my arms.

"Why did you never put the ad for my truck in the paper?"

I eye him suspiciously. "I thought you needed relationship advice."

"I do. But *that* first."

I try my best to hide my smile. "I forgot."

"It's your job, Vannah. You didn't forget."

I shrug. "I don't think you should sell it."

I glance up at him. There's a crooked grin on his face now.

"It's a good truck," I say. "It still runs. You should keep it."

His crooked grin turns knowing, all of a sudden, and I'm not quite sure if I'm thankful or wary of that.

"Anyway. What's your relationship question?"

He gets quiet and goes to biting the inside of his cheek.

"She thinks I love you."

Suddenly, I feel the color in my face draining into the gray sidewalk at our feet.

"What?"

"She thinks I love you," he repeats, but this time, slower. "Like, really love you."

We walk a few more steps in our silence.

"Why?" It's all I can think to ask. "Why does she think that?"

"I don't know...because you've been my friend all my life, because I talk about you, because you're here..."

"Wait." I stop and face him. "Why do you talk about me to her?"

He shrugs and stops, too. "Why wouldn't I?"

I let go of some air I think I had been holding deep inside my chest.

"Well, did you tell her we're just friends?"

He doesn't say anything. He doesn't even move. He just keeps his head down, his eyes on the sidewalk.

The conversation is getting awkward fast. I don't know what he's thinking. I have no idea what to say.

"Okay," I say, starting to walk again. "Tell her... Tell her you love her. Tell her you'd choose her over me every day for the rest of your life."

I hate my words. But I love him more.

He's walking too, now, but he's also shaking his head slowly back and forth.

"What?" I ask.

"I can't tell her that."

"What? Why?"

He seems to ignore my question.

"You're seeing Jake Buckler, aren't you?"

His mood has shifted. He seems agitated, all of a sudden.

"What?"

"Jake," he says. "You're seeing him."

I narrow my eyes. "Yes, we went on a date. But that's not really any of your business."

He pushes out a fake laugh. "Vannah, you've been my business since Day One."

We get to the door of the office, and we both stop while I root in my purse for the keys.

"Salem, go talk to your girlfriend." The word *girlfriend* comes out of my mouth sounding as if it's a four-letter word. It surprises even me. I don't think I meant it to.

He lets go of a sigh, just as I'm getting the door open. Then he follows me inside and sets the bag onto the front counter.

"Go," I say, facing him.

"Okay, okay. I'm going."

"And tell her," I say, a little too angrily.

He meets my gaze, and something in his eyes asks me: *Why? Why are you upset?* I ignore it, though. And after several moments, he tips his cap and then turns to leave.

And a second later, he's slipping out the door.

I watch him from the window.

I really wish I knew more about what was going on in his head these days. I used to know that; I used to be able to read his mind.

But I do know that he loves her. He loves Anna. It hurts to admit it. It hurts to see him love someone else. But what can I do? I'm the reason we didn't talk for six years. I'm the one who never wrote him back. And anyway, I keep telling myself that if he loved me, he wouldn't be with her. No matter what he says or doesn't say, if he loved me, he'd be with me.

I watch him get into his truck in front of the grocery store, two parking lots away. Then after a second, the truck reverses, and my eyes follow it down the street, until I can't see it anymore.

I should probably start taking my own advice.

"The train is gone," I whisper under my breath.

I should move on.

Chapter Thirty-Four

Savannah
(23 Years Old)

"Pizza delivery."

I hear two knocks on the door, and it makes me jump. But then, before I know it, I'm flying off the couch and standing in front of the mirror in the hall.

I smooth back my hair and smile, making sure there's nothing in my teeth, before heading to the door. But I get halfway there, and I stop.

There's a vampire book sitting on the table. And I'm not quite sure why, but I feel the need to hide it.

I pick up the book and stuff it in between *Anne of Green Gables* and *The Great Gatsby* on the bookshelf.

And as I'm walking back to the door, I notice the Polaroids are gone. I thought for sure I had put them underneath that book.

I hear another knock, and I forget all about the photos and rush toward it.

"Hi," I say, opening the door to a handsome man.

"One large pepperoni pizza," he says, smiling back at me.

"Thank you." I take the pizza and start to close the door.

"What?" He puts his hand to the door. "No tip?"

I laugh. "Where are my manners?" I shove my hand into my jeans pocket and pull out an old gum wrapper.

"Will this do?" I ask, holding the wrapper out.

He looks at it and shakes his head while a devilish grin plays on his face. Something about his look makes me swoon.

"Not even close. And even if that were real money, it wouldn't be any good."

"No?" I ask, pretending to be surprised.

Jake steps inside, forcing me to step back. And then he takes the pizza box and sets it down onto the little table in the hall.

"No," he repeats.

He comes closer and puts his arms around me. I momentarily close my eyes and breathe in his crisp, exotic-smelling cologne. I could swear sometimes he's just stepped off some jet from Bora Bora right before he comes to see me.

But this is the first time he's ever touched me like this. And I like it.

I wrap my arms around his neck and press my body into his embrace. He holds me for a long while.

And then he pulls away and looks into my eyes. And there's a moment—like a question—that floats in the air between us.

Can I kiss you?

I don't know if it's him or me that asks it. Regardless, I answer, by keeping my stare in his.

He moves closer, his lips nearly touching mine. The way he does it makes me lose my breath. He's so deliberate in his actions, yet also so careful, as he takes a strand of my hair and tucks it behind my ear. It's as if I'm standing in front of two men.

Within a moment, his warm breaths hit my lips, and instinctively, my eyes fall shut.

My heart races. I almost can't breathe. His lips touch mine. A shock resonates through my body.

The kiss is new, foreign, different, amazing. And too soon, it's over, and he's pressing his forehead to mine.

"I'm sorry," he breathes out. "I just couldn't wait a second longer to do that."

I laugh softly. "I'm just wondering who got the tip."

"I did." I hear him smile. "I definitely got the tip."

Then he pulls me into his arms again.

"I never expected to find you here, Savannah."

I rest my head on his chest and speak softly: "You're not what I expected to find here, either."

And he's not. He's not at all what I expected. What I expected to find here was a boy I fell in love with when I was just a little girl. I expected a boy who would hold my hand while we watched the sky light up in a summer storm; I expected a boy who would lie next to me on Hogan's slab and fall asleep to the sound of the

creek water pushing through the concrete; and I
expected a boy who I thought would always be mine.

But that boy is gone now. That boy grew up. And
now, he's a man in love with another woman.

But this man in front of me—he's beautiful and
loving and funny, and I can't find anything wrong with
him. This man just might be my future. In fact, I'd be
lucky if he were. And I'm afraid that if I don't let go of
that boy from my past, that I might miss out on
everything good that could be waiting for me—on this
side of my crystal ball.

Chapter Thirty-Five

Savannah
(23 Years Old)

Day 6,657

"You're better off trying to freeze hell."

"What?" I ask, looking up.

"That wallpaper there has never seen daylight."

"Well, there's a first for everything." I stand up and take a stack of papers to the desk. Salem comes over and takes another stack and sets it on the desk, too.

"Plus, apparently, there's a safe under all this." I gesture toward the corner still full of black and white news articles, long ago, folded into newspapers.

Salem takes off his hat and runs his fingers over his hair. "Is this how he hid it all these years?"

I laugh. "I guess so."

"Well, what's in it?"

"I don't know." I shake my head. "Safe stuff. The original deed, maybe, papers... Things like that."

Immediately, he gives me a sideways look. "You're not thinking about selling, are you?"

"No. No," I assure him. "I just thought it might be good to actually know where the important stuff is. Thought that might be a good thing."

"Yeah, that's probably a good thing," he agrees, refitting his cap over his head. "I'll help ya."

He moves toward the stack of newspapers and bends down low next to me. I can feel his face so close to mine. And I think he notices it, too. We both stop and surrender to our breathing. For a solid three seconds, all I can hear is the rasping of our breaths and the beating of my heart as the air around us grows thick.

And then he moves. He lifts a stack of papers into his arms and carries them to my desk. And the moment is lost.

My heart is pounding in my chest, but I try not to think about it. I force myself to move, and I pick up an armful of papers. But at the same time, I steal a quick glance at him. If he was affected at all, he's got a good poker face. It almost makes me think I was only just imagining things.

We get all the papers moved from the corner to my desk. And now my desk is full of newspapers, and our hands are covered in black ink. But now there's also a safe—a black safe—in plain view, staring back at us.

I kneel down and pull on the little door.

It doesn't budge.

"Do you have the key?"

I breathe out a defeated sigh. "No."

Salem laughs loudly and then plops down into my desk chair. Meanwhile, I twist around and let my back fall against the wall.

"He never said where the key was," I say. "I think I just always hoped it was open or something...or that I would have found the key by now."

"Well, I guess I could try and open it back at the shop. I hear they're mostly meant to be firesafe, not necessarily theftproof."

I bite my bottom lip in thought. "Yeah," I murmur, considering it. I slide down the wall, until I'm resting on my heels. "You don't mind?"

He shakes his head. "No, I can try."

"All right." I glance at the little safe and then back at Salem. "Thank you."

He smiles, and out of nowhere, a pesky thought crosses my mind.

"Why are people warning me about you?"

"What?" He looks a little taken aback.

I don't say anything. I just wait for him to talk.

He sits back in the chair and lowers his head, so that I can't see his face behind his red baseball cap.

"In high school," he says, "when you didn't write back...and after I called, and I texted..."

My heart drops in my chest.

"When I didn't hear back from you," he goes on, "I kind of lost it for a little while. And the last couple months of senior year, I just..." He shrugs his shoulders. "The season had just ended, and I didn't have basketball to distract me anymore. And I started drinking. I stayed out too late. I skipped class."

His eyes meet mine. They're dark and thoughtful now.

"The thing they're all talking about—the reason why they probably warned you to stay away from me— besides the fact that I suck at being a boyfriend because I spend all my time on Sheppard's Hill..."

My eyes dart to him, and he stops, almost as if he knows he's said too much.

"Anyway," he goes on, without addressing the Sheppard's Hill part, "today, they all have their stories and reasons for why I'm not all right, but it's all because of one night."

He pauses and refits his cap over his head. I don't say anything. I wouldn't know what to say anyway. I just wait for him to continue. And he does, eventually.

"One night, I got drunk, and I got in my truck, and I drove down Excelsior, and I ran right into the side of the Old Red Bridge."

I suck in a gasp, and my hand covers my mouth. "Eben."

"No," he says, shaking his head, "I was fine. And no one was with me. It was the stupidest thing I've ever done, but by the grace of God, I was fine."

He sits up straighter in the chair.

"My truck got a little beat up. The bridge got more beat up. And thankfully, for my ass, Sheriff Howard showed up. So no criminal record. But that was the last straw for my parents. I was basically on house arrest with them until I finished high school. And then, as soon as they could, they shipped me off to college. And believe it or not, it took me four years, but I got it mostly together there."

I feel his eyes on me, but I don't look at him. My stare is concentrated on a tiny piece of the carpet. I don't know what to say. I got so caught up in the story that I missed how it all began. But now, I remember.

"But that's why," he says. "That's why they all think I'm a little bit of trouble."

He's quiet then.

"I'm really not, though," he adds, in a rasping voice. "Trouble," he clarifies.

My stare slowly lifts to his.

"I'm sorry."

"No." He shakes his head. "No. It wasn't your fault."

"But if I would have just..."

"No," he says, cutting me off. "You did what you thought you had to do. I was responsible for me."

I silently stare into his eyes. I want to take back everything—everything I didn't do back then. I want to write him. I want to call him. I want his eighteen-year-old self to know how hard it was to let him go. I want him to know how many nights I cried for him and how many days I walked through as if I were in a fog, missing him.

"It wasn't your fault," he assures me, giving me a gentle smile.

My eyes drop to the floor. A handful of emotions are spiraling through my body, and since I can't choose just one, I swear they vow to tear up every part of me.

"I'll see if I can get this open." He slowly stands and moves toward the safe. And then in one, smooth motion, he lifts it off the floor.

My eyes find his, and I just nod, unable to do much else.

"I'll call you and let you know," he says. Then, he disappears into the front of the little building.

Seconds later, I hear the bell above the door clanging. And soon, it's just me, left sorting out a decision I made six years ago. If I would have known how it was all going to affect him, I would have done it all differently.

I thought I was saving him. And this whole time, I was killing him.

Chapter Thirty-Six

Salem
(23 Years Old)

Day 6,659

"Damn," I say, under my breath.

I'm in the back office of the lumberyard, and I've been staring at this safe for about ten minutes now, trying to figure out what's the best way to go about this.

I've got a drill, and I'm hoping that just drilling through the lock will work. I'd rather not have to cut through its hinges.

I push out a puff of air and narrow my eyes at it. "Well. I guess, here goes nothin'."

I lean over to pick up the drill, and my chain falls

from the neck of my shirt and dangles in front of me. I go to tuck it back in, when my fingers hit the key, and I stop.

I stop, and I stare at that key.

Then I stare at the lock.

Could it be?

It's a long shot, but maybe. Vannah did give it to me when she was hanging out at the paper. It's worth a try, I guess.

I pull the chain over my head and put the key to the lock.

And I push.

It slides in.

I carefully turn it.

It turns.

And just like that, the safe clicks open.

"Well, that was easy."

I laugh to myself and pull open the door. It doesn't open easily, and its hinges scream as they come back to life after maybe decades of resting.

I wiggle the key out of the lock and go to close the little door again, when something falls out.

It's a photo. I pick it up and go to put it back in the safe, but I stop when I notice the woman in the picture. I've seen her before. I think about it for a second. I've seen her before at Lester's house. She was the girl in the frame.

I turn the photo over. There's something written on the back. I read it. And then slowly, gradually—like a slow-burning oak—something deep inside me starts to stir.

Chapter Thirty-Seven

Savannah
(23 Years Old)

"Tell me what you were like when you were little."

I smile, and Jake pulls me closer. I can feel the fire rising up in me, starting at the place his fingertips graze the bare skin of my arm.

It's Tuesday. We're on my couch, barely watching an old episode of *Friends*.

"What do you mean?" I ask.

"I don't know. Just, what were you like? Were you shy? Were you awkward? Did you ever get in trouble?"

I tilt my head back to think about it.

"I don't think I was shy. I liked sports, volleyball mostly. I was awkward sometimes. If I wanted to do something, I usually did it. But I stayed out of trouble, mostly, I think."

"Aah." He nods his head.

"What about you. What were you like?"

"Well." He looks off for a moment. "I don't think most people would call me shy, but I was."

His other hand comes to rest on my knee, and I watch as he mindlessly traces a white scar on my skin.

"And both my parents were lawyers, so everyone thought I was smart. And I did okay in school; I just had to work hard for it, I guess. Math and science were two things that didn't come easy to me."

I laugh. "But can you write a sentence?"

"I can," he says, proudly.

"Well, that's really all you need in my book."

He laughs and plants a kiss on my forehead. I pause to take in the way his lips linger on my skin. And then he pulls away and looks into my eyes.

"I like you," he says.

My gaze falls briefly before returning to his.

"I like you, too."

His face lights up. And then he takes my hand, and I rest my head on his chest. And for several moments, we're just still. But I can't stop smiling because the truth is, I don't know *that* much about him, but I *do* already like him. He's easy to like. And I'm okay with *like* right now. I can do *like*.

"Do you have any brothers or sisters?"

"Mm hmm," he hums. "One brother. Older. Lives in Chester. Married to his high school sweetheart."

"Aw," I say.

"Yeah, they're sickeningly happy."

I laugh.

"What about you?" he asks.

"One sister. Whitney. She's back in South Carolina and works at a public relations firm."

"Aah, are you guys close?"

"Um, yeah. We're closer than we used to be. She's only two years older, but I was always too young for her and her friends." I smile up at him. "But she eventually got over that."

"That's good to hear."

He intertwines his fingers with mine.

"Did you play any sports?" I ask.

"Hockey."

My eyes dart to his mouth. "But you have teeth."

He chuckles. "I wore a face mask."

"But what about this?" I say, delicately tracing with my fingertips a fine, white scar on his jawline.

"That would be the work of Henry Waterfeld." He laughs. "We were playing roller hockey in the cul-de-sac. I just got a little too close to his high-stick."

My eyes grow wide.

"It was nothing, really. The scar itself is much more exciting than its story."

I watch him then, as he rubs his jaw with his thumb and forefinger. His eyes are somewhere far off, as if he's thinking back, maybe. But there's something about his thoughtful expression that makes me feel as if he has so many more stories to tell.

"I bet you made one very cute hockey player."

His gaze falls, and he blushes. But when his eyes return to mine, he's smiling.

"I wish I could have been a fly on *your* wall when you were growing up," he says.

I narrow my eyes at him and push my lips to one

side. "I probably would have squished you. I'm not a fan of bugs."

"I don't know," he says, shaking his head. "I never told you I used to be fast, did I?"

"Really?"

"Well, on skates, anyway."

"Okay, you win. I don't think I ever could have brought myself to squish a skates-wearing fly."

He leans his head back and laughs. Meanwhile, I rest my cheek on the inside of his shoulder.

"Why did you move here?" I ask, after his laughter fades.

I feel his shoulder lift slightly.

"I have an aunt who works in St. Louis. I liked the area, but I'm not big on the city life. So, one day, I just drove. I drove down *44* and then turned off onto *100*. And I stopped at the first place that felt like home. And that place was here."

I look up at him.

"This feels like Popeye's home?"

"Yeah," he says, "this feels like Popeye's home."

I softly laugh. "Well, I'm happy you stopped here."

He pulls me even closer and gently rests his head on mine.

"Really?"

"Yeah. You're a really nice surprise."

His fingers are now gently caressing my bare arm, leaving a tingly sensation in their wake. It feels good. It feels good to be in his arms. And it's hard to explain, but everything he does feels as if it's a promise—a promise of safety and protection and love. And I believe it. I know it's early. And I know it's crazy, but I believe in all those things in his arms.

"Savannah."

"Hmm?"

I lift my eyes to his.

"I could get used to this," he says, in a low rasp.

There's a smile on his face. And it instantly makes my heart feel full. And I know... I know, with a certainty I've never had before, that it's because I could get used to this, too. I could get used to days in my porch swing, getting to know him more and more with every new story from his past. I could get used to nights on the couch, with him always making sure I have enough of the blanket to keep me warm. I could get used to his passionate kisses, his touch, the way he says my name like no one's ever said it—as if it's a word from his favorite song.

I could get used to Jake Buckler.

I could easily fall for Jake Buckler.

And just maybe...just maybe, I already have.

Chapter Thirty-Eight

Savannah
(23 Years Old)

Day 6,677

"I'm sitting at my desk at the office when I hear a knock on the door. It's late. I find sometimes it's best to work at night. There's fewer distractions that way.

I stand up and cautiously walk out into the main room. The door's locked. And there's probably no good reason why someone should be knocking on it right about now.

I glance at the baseball bat in the corner. I bought it after the first night I spent in here writing until three in the morning. I never intended to use it—the crime section in this town usually entails the latest police force's rant about not parking on the grass downtown or reminding kids that curfew is midnight.

Nevertheless, I feel my heart rate speed up. Outside, it's a starless sky—cloudy and the blackest of dark. I know it because I stepped outside just an hour ago to get some fresh air.

I get halfway across the room and try to make out the dark figure through the glass on the other side of the door.

"Savannah. It's Salem." I hear the voice before I'm even able to make anything else out.

"Salem?"

I'm relieved it's just him; I feel my heart start to slow again.

I get the door open, and he just stands there—stiff and disheveled. His hair is a little longer than usual, and it's sticking out every which way from under a red, faded baseball cap. There are shadows under his eyes, and his stare is directed toward his sawdust-covered work boots. And he's holding the safe.

I back up to let him in the door.

"What's wrong?"

He shakes his head but doesn't say anything.

I'm a little thrown off. I glance at the black and white clock on the wall. It reads *1:10*.

I get the door closed behind him. Meanwhile, he goes straight back to my office and sets the safe down in its place in the corner of the room.

"I got it open."

He's already sitting in the blue recliner when I join him in my office.

"Really?" I go to the safe. "How?"

"It wasn't a problem."

I look up at him, and he smiles for the first time

tonight.

"Turns out, I had the key."

I glance at the unharmed safe, and then quickly, my stare is back on him.

He's dangling his chain with the key at the end of it from his fingers.

"No," I say, in disbelief.

He sets the chain onto the corner of my desk.

"*That* key was for *this* safe?" I ask, pointing first at the key and then at the safe.

"Yep."

"Huh." I stare at the little safe. "I had no idea."

I'm silent for a second, as I bite at my bottom lip, trying to remember the day I found the key.

"I hope Uncle Lester wasn't looking for it this whole time. I found it in the broom closet. I thought it was just some old key. Now, I feel bad."

"Nah," he says, shaking his head. "He just might have known I had it."

My eyes find his.

"What do you mean?"

"He saw me wearing it once."

"He did?"

"Yeah, when we were in high school—when you came back from South Carolina that summer."

"Wait. Was there something in there? Is that why you're here?"

He shakes his head, even before I get it all out.

"No, no." He takes off his cap and runs his fingers through his messy curls and then sighs.

"But you have to tell me," he says.

"What?"

"I know you've been seeing Jake Buckler. I saw you guys out last weekend."

I sit down on the floor next to the safe, bring my knees up to my chest and press my back against the wall.

"Okay," I say.

He seems distracted.

"I think I'm in love with you."

Everything in me freezes up—my muscles, my words, my thoughts.

"You *think*...you're in love with me?"

"I think I know..." He stops.

I'm breathing. I know I'm breathing—only because I can feel my chest moving. But I'm not getting any air. I push myself up from the floor and walk to the door—if only just to get a breath.

"I know...," he says. "I know this is crazy."

I glance at the clock. *1:15.*

"Anna? Does she...?"

He averts his gaze to the brown, speckled carpet.

"She doesn't know I'm here." He anxiously rubs the back of his neck.

"Salem." I sullenly breathe out his name.

"I know. I know this is a stretch, but I just... I just don't want any regrets. If we have a chance... If there's a chance, Vannah, for you and me..."

My eyes slowly find the floor. This moment, it feels so raw, as if I tried to touch it, it would bleed. This is what I wanted. When I was twelve, *this* is what I wanted. When I was sixteen, *this* is what I wanted. When I got back here, *this* is what I wanted. *He* is what I wanted. But tonight, it just feels wrong, as if we're trying to fit the sun into the moon.

"At least, we can give it a chance, Vannah."

I find his eyes. They're soft and sincere, and they're pleading with me. I want to say *yes*. I want to scream it as loud as I can. But I don't.

"Can I ask you something?" I ask.

"Yeah, sure, anything."

"Is this because of Jake? Are you here because of him?"

His eyes descend to his boots. And then there's silence.

His quiet is a knife to my heart. And from somewhere I hear the words of my grandmother float into my mind like an ominous cloud. *Love and jealousy are not the same. When love fades, love still remains. When jealousy fades, love does not remain.*

"Come on, Vannah, it's not like you see yourself falling for this guy."

I don't look at him.

Seconds trudge on.

"Vannah. You can't see yourself falling in love with him. Can you?"

The moments tick out on that clock. *One. Two. Three.* But then I feel my stare slowly wandering up. And before we get to *four*, my eyes find his and rest there.

Four.

Five.

"Wow," he says, as if understanding is gradually washing over him.

"Salem, it's not..." I stop, suddenly at a loss for words. "He *is* a great guy, but this is just..."

"Who do you choose, Vannah?"

I meet his gaze. It's turned cold. His eyes are raging—a desert storm, spewing sand and wind.

I'm speechless. I don't know what to say. I don't know how to react to his coolness.

"I just need to know," he says, leaning forward in

222

the recliner. He rubs his eyes and then brings a fist to his mouth.

A moment drags out between us, as if it's a cinder block being pulled in the mud by a rope.

"Salem, I can't do what you're asking me to do. I can't choose. Not like this."

The color in his face drains, until his almond skin is the shade of sand. And I watch him, as his eyes catch on the rotary phone on my desk, the printer in the corner, the door. He does everything to avoid making eye contact with me.

"So, that's it, I guess." He slowly rises from the old, blue chair. "I guess that's my answer."

I try to swallow down the tears that I know are just waiting to fall.

"Salem," I plead.

Silence—his eyes lost in mine.

It's almost as if we both suspect that just a small sound will cause us to dissolve into nothingness. And I know, deep down, there's not a word I could say that will heal this moment. The silence has already done its damage. It's just like right after a storm—when the wind's died down and there are branches strewn every which way in the dirt. All that's left is the cleanup.

He hesitates but then walks past me. The familiar scent of his cologne floats in the air, triggering my memories of him. And suddenly, I smell creek water and the synthetic canvas of his old trampoline. And I can feel sawdust running through my fingers and the beat of his heart against my cheek. And there's a part of me that wants to beg him to stay.

The tears begin filling up behind my eyelids. I feel as if my heart is ripping in two. One piece is going with him while one piece is staying, remaining faithful to

Jake. And all the while, my mind is foggy, clouded with so many thoughts: *Why is he here? Why now? What if he's just jealous? What if, in the next few minutes, he realizes he made a mistake—that he's still in love with Anna?*

He needs some time to think about this.

I want him to love me—but not like this.

The tears stream down my cheeks, but I don't even have the strength to wipe them away.

I can feel his stare burning into me, although I refuse to look up.

"You asked me once if I could rewind time for you—make us see what we didn't see before."

His words force my eyes to lift, just as his gaze casts down.

"Well, I did," he says, setting a folded piece of paper onto the counter.

He looks into my eyes then, for what feels as if it's an eternity. It's painful, as if he's slowly cutting off his piece of my heart with a blunt knife. It's his *good-bye*. I know it is.

And then, he turns. And that little bell above the door rings the warning that he's gone.

I tell myself it's not *for good*.

I wish I could believe it.

Chapter Thirty-Nine

Savannah
(23 Years Old)

Day 6,677

After a few minutes of shell shock, my eyes catch on the piece of paper Salem left on the counter. I can't even imagine what's on it.

Slowly, I move toward it. My hands are shaking. My tears are still falling. I'm trying my best to swallow them down.

I take the note and fall into a chair in the corner of the room. And carefully, I force the page open.

It's his handwriting. It scrolls and winds down the page in black ink.

I take a breath, and then with a cautious heart, I

read his blurry words:

Day 4,592

"Vannah?"

"Hmm?"

"Are you sleeping?" I ask.

"Mm hmm."

"But you just answered me," I say.

"Mm hmm," you say again.

I smile and let my head rest back on the wooden boards of the dock.

"My heart's awake," you mumble.

I lift my head, rest my eyes on your face and just watch you.

"My heart's awake, daydreaming of you," you add.

I smile. And then I kiss your hair and push strands back from your eyes.

Your eyes open.

"I love you, Vannah," I whisper. "And not just like a friend. I'm in love with you. And someday, I want to marry you, and I want to find our star tower, and I want to grow old with you. But, Vannah?"

"Mm hmm?" you say.

"Most of all, I love you."

And you smile at me.

"I love you, too," you whisper.

Day 4,563

"Do you have to go back?"

I hear you smile before I even hear a word. "Not now."

"Ever?" I ask.

You don't say anything, at first.

"I'm coming with you," I say. "And if I can't live there, I'm going to visit you...a lot."

"*Eben,*" *you protest, "it might as well be a world away. Plus, you belong here.*"

"*No,*" *I say. "I belong wherever you are.*"

Day 4,562

"*Eben, what are you doing here?*" *you ask.*

I shrug. "I heard you were back in town."

"*Come here,*" *you say. "Come up here.*"

I make my way down the stone walk and slowly up the three wooden porch steps to your uncle's door.

"*Vannah,*" *I say, "I've missed you. And I don't care if you've got a boyfriend. Someday soon you're gonna find out he's not the guy for you. I'm in love with you, Vannah. And I know you love me, too.*"

Day 4,023

You turn my way. You've just asked me if I could, would I choose a spot on the moon or one right next to you.

"*I'd stay right here,*" *I tell you.*

"*But you could see the world, literally,*" *you say.*

I shrug it off. "You're my world."

Day 3,650

"*Vannah, can I talk to you?*" *I don't even acknowledge Rylan Tennessee.*

You look at me with a question written on your face. "Okay," *you say.*

I watch as you turn your attention back to Rylan. "I'll call you after practice," *you say to him. And then you smile.*

He glances at me before he turns to leave. We're eye to eye for only a split-second, but I know exactly what he said—because I said the same thing.

She's mine.

"What did you want to talk about?" you ask, when he's gone.

"What?" I stutter. "That? Was what?"

You laugh at my jumbled words. "What are you trying to say?" you ask.

"I just...," I start again, reorganizing my thoughts. "I just wanted you to know that you're going to see soon that Rylan Tennessee is not the guy for you. And when you do, I'll be here, and we'll have a month full of late nights and long talks and stolen kisses. It'll be a beautiful month, but it'll be just another beautiful month in between all the beautiful months we'll share in this life. Because I love you, Vannah. I always have. I always will. And I'll do my best to make sure you always know that."

Day 3,285

"Vannah?"

You turn and face me. "Yeah?"

"Can I ask you something?" I ask.

"Yeah," you say.

"Do you like me?" I ask. "Because I like you. I've liked you for a long time now. I just thought you should know that."

Day 2,920

"Do you think we can see it yet?" you ask.

I shrug. "Maybe."

I run to my bed and start crawling over you to get to the window.

"Watch it," you say. "Your pokey elbows are stabbing my ribs."

Your voice makes me stop. My body hovers over yours. I make a joke about my elbows not being pokey. And then I look into your eyes. And I see something. I see

228

your secret. And instead of continuing to the window, I move my mouth closer to yours, and I press my lips to your lips.

Our first kiss.

Day 1,095

"You love her, don't you?" Dillon asks.

I turn to you and smile.

"I'm only eight," I say to you, "and I don't know anything about love. But I do know that, of all the girls, you're my favorite."

And I give you a hug, just so you know it's true. And I don't care what Dillon has to say about it.

Then I whisper in your ear: "You'll always be my favorite girl. And if someday you find yourself believing something different, it's a lie."

Day 1

"Who are you?" you ask.

"Salem." I clear my throat. "My name is Salem Ebenezer."

"Ebenezer?"

I nod.

"Do people call you Eben?"

I shake my head. "No, but you can."

"What are you doing here anyway?" you ask.

"I noticed you a few days ago, and I've been coming here ever since. You look nice, like we could be friends, and maybe someday, when we're grown-ups, we could be more."

"Okay," you say.

"Vannah?"

"Yeah?" you ask.

"Are you mine?"

You give me a pretty smile. "Yes," you say.

"Eben?"
"Yeah?" I ask.
"Are you mine?"
"Always," I say.

I press the page to my chest. My hands have stilled. There's a smile on my lips, but my heart is still breaking and the tears are still falling. I long for those moments—those simple, delicate, precious moments when the sky was darker and the stars, brighter.

I want them back. I want to hold them in my hands. I want to feel them. I want to press them against my heart.

I close my eyes and pray for them. I pray that somewhere, somehow, those moments are being held in a safe, happy place—where no one can touch them. Those are *our* moments. They'll always be ours—*only ours.*

I wipe my eyes with the back of my hand.

They're only ours.

And even if there is no safe place they can go, and even if, by now, they're nothing but lost pieces of dust—floating in the light of an empty room—I still love them.

I still remember them.

I still love them.

I always will.

Chapter Forty

Savannah
(23 Years Old)

Day 6,692

I'm sitting at the little writer's desk in my house when a glare hits the window. I watch it dance to the wood floor. And then I see an old pickup truck ambling down the drive.

It's Salem.

Instantly, the pen in my hand falls to the surface of the desk, and without another thought, I suck in a quick breath. Seconds disappear into the hum of his truck's engine. And then it's quiet. And I hear the hinges of his door scream before I stand and make my way out to the porch.

It's been two weeks since I last saw him in my office at one in the morning. And I think I've spent the last two weeks secretly soul-searching...and praying— praying that after some time, he might still feel what he felt that night.

The wooden floorboards feel coarse under my bare feet as I go to the big porch brace and lean up against it.

He stops when he sees me.

"Hey," he says, closing the door to his truck.

"Hi." I'm so nervous, but I'm also so happy to see him.

He forces his hands into his jeans pockets, bows his head and shifts his weight to his other leg.

"I'm going to ask Anna to marry me."

I stop breathing. He meets my gaze, but I quickly look away, and at the same time, I rest my hand on the brace.

"Vannah."

I don't say anything. I just force myself to take a breath. And then I move toward the porch swing and fall into it.

There's a bird in the tree beside me. It distracts me for a moment. It's singing as if it's just another sunny day.

Salem walks to the porch and presses his back against the brace.

"Savannah, I'm telling you this because you're my oldest friend. And if for no other reason, you should know. And you should hear it from me."

I breathe out—slowly, steadily—but I still don't say a word. I just keep staring at that little bird in the tree while all my hopes of a life with this boy run out of me and pool up on the weathered boards at my feet.

"And I know," he goes on. "I know that just a

couple weeks ago I was asking you..." He stops there, and his silence has my eyes wandering to his.

"Vannah, she loves me. And I *do* love her. And I know the timing is all messed up. But this date—the day I was going to ask her—was planned months before you got here. And then, you got here... And then, it just..."

He stops and drops his gaze.

"It just all went to hell when you got here," he finishes. "But I'm trying to put it all back together again. I'm trying to put my life back together—the way it was before you... The way it was before you came back."

He stops again. And this time, his hand goes to the back of his neck. And he sighs; he sighs, as if all the wind leaves his sails—in that one, solitary moment.

"And I came here to tell you that I'm sorry, too. I just let my imagination get the best of me, that's all. I'm sorry for what I said. I'm sorry to even ask you something like that...like I did. I shouldn't have. I had no business coming in there like that. That wasn't fair to you...or anyone."

He exhales. And I think maybe he waits for me to say something. But I don't. I *can't*. And he goes on.

"I just got caught up in the past, I guess. I just got caught up dreaming an old dream; that's all. And I..." He pauses and clears his throat. "I think maybe, maybe you were right—what you said a while back, when we were younger. I think the universe *did* just intend for us to be friends."

And then he's quiet. And for a minute, I listen to that bird sing in the tree.

"Savannah?"

I sit back in the swing.

"Maybe," I whisper.

Then, I stare at that bird, secretly asking it to sing a song that will make this all go away.

"Do you forgive me, for being an idiot?"

I look up at him and into his light brown eyes. And there's a thought that flashes through my mind: *this might really be* the end.

"I forgive you," I whisper.

He nods. But then he remains still for several, silent seconds before he starts to turn.

"Salem."

I wait until he's facing me again. And when I lock eyes with him, suddenly I don't know what to say.

I love you.

I. Love. You.

This isn't how this is supposed to go.

You're supposed to choose me.

You're supposed to love me.

We were supposed to be together.

In the end, it was supposed to be me *and* you.

Eben, I love you.

I don't know how long I'm in his eyes when, somehow, I recall that the moments have just kept moving—and I haven't said a word.

But he *loves* her.

I drop my gaze and press my lips together.

"Thanks for rewinding time."

I say it despite the fact that I want to hate him. I want to hate him for closing the door on eighteen years, woven together with *our* tears and *our* laughter and *our* moments. I want to hate him, but I can't.

He hesitates but then nods once.

"Do you think if it all would have happened that way, we'd be in a different place right now? That we wouldn't be better off *just* friends?"

234

I lift my shoulders and then let them fall.

"No tellin'," I say. I know the words come out sounding sad.

He holds my stare for longer than he should. And then he slowly tips his cap.

"Take care, Vannah."

There's a heartbeat where the world, as I know it, falls away. And then, I feel my lips move.

"You too, Eben."

My eyes follow him as he makes his way back down the three porch steps and to his old truck.

There's a part of me that wants to run to him and tell him that he's wrong, that maybe we're both wrong—about everything.

I hear the door to his truck squeak open. And then, I watch him climb into the cab.

"Stay," I whisper, under my breath, knowing that he can't hear me.

Maybe we're wrong.

His truck slowly reverses down the driveway, shifting ever so slightly as it moves over the big, white rocks.

And then, all too soon, he hits the county road and takes off. But not before he looks back.

Maybe we're wrong.

My heart starts to race, though I was sure he took it with him. I force my hand to my chest to slow it down. And gradually, I feel my eyes start to burn with tears. But I can't tell if I'm mourning the loss of my oldest friendship...or my happily-ever-after.

Salem left town a month later. He never told me

he was leaving. Joey, from the lumberyard, said he moved to some little town in Iowa. He said they were opening another store up there. But that's all he knew.

Rumor has it that Anna went with him. And unlike most rumors around here, I assume this one's probably true because I haven't seen her around either.

I thought about selling the paper and moving back to South Carolina. I thought it might just be easier that way. But as quickly as the thought came into my mind, it vanished. My uncle chose this paper over the love of his life. I couldn't stand to see it be all for nothing. Plus, I like it here. This is home. And no matter how much I miss the beach and the ocean and the salty breeze, I belong here. I belong with this old creek water and the tall sycamores and the soft, red clay. And even though I know Jake would have gone with me, I also know he belongs here, too.

Jake and I have been seeing each other for five months now. He keeps asking me about rings and houses and churches. They're indirect questions, but we both know that I know what they mean.

I can picture myself with Jake. He's a good, solid, beautiful man, who loves his nephews and baseball and the simple things—even though he looks like a piece of art. I love that contradiction about him.

And I love him. I do. I thank God for him every day.

And every day, I try to think of Salem less and less. He's in so many memories; it's hard *not* to think of him. But I do suppose one day will come when his name doesn't cross my mind. *Someday. Maybe.*

Chapter Forty-One

Savannah
(23 Years Old)

Day 6,862

I kneel down to the old safe in the corner of my office and use Salem's key to open it. I hadn't really looked through it since the night he brought it back.

I sift through several envelopes—one holding the deed; another, some old insurance papers; and still another, a passport. I take out the passport. Uncle Lester's photo is inside. It expired ten years ago, and there are no stamps on its pages. I close the passport and set it gently back into the envelope, when I stop and notice a small photo. It's stuck in between two folders.

I carefully pick it up. It looks old. Its edges are worn, and a piece of the top corner is slightly torn off.

I stare into the photo and at the woman in it. It's Olivia.

Uncle Lester talked about her all the time. She's young in the photo, maybe twenty-something, but I still recognize her. She's not that much older in this photo than she was in the photo Uncle Les always kept in a frame in his living room.

She's beautiful, with long auburn hair and freckles dotting her nose and cheeks. I know my uncle had some regrets in life. He was very open about them. And I know one of those regrets was her—not in loving her, but in letting her get away.

I smile at the photo, and then I flip it over and carefully place it on top of the stack of folders.

But then, I stop.

There's handwriting on the back, and my eyes immediately go to those three little words:

Change our story.

I stare at the words. And just like a breaking wave, a sinking feeling gains momentum and then all at once crashes into my chest. It feels like panic. I panic for Olivia.

I turn the photo over.

"How could it all have turned out that way?" I ask the woman in the photo. "You both loved each other."

The young woman's stoic expression doesn't change; her eyes are caught on something off in the distance, as if she doesn't have an answer to my question.

I lower myself to the floor and lean my back

against the wall.

"Why did it have to end that way, Olivia?"

I look deep into the faded photo, pleading with her.

"Wasn't there something you could have done?"

You loved him. And he loved you. He never married; he loved you that much. His heart belonged to you. He'd never give it to someone else.

I let my hand with the photo in it fall to my side, and I stare out the window.

He loved you, Olivia. And that's the song he was going to go out singing—that's the last song he ever sang. And that was enough for him. Your song was enough for him.

My panicked heart starts to ache, that kind of ache that wishes it had a voice, so that it could cry out.

I close my eyes to push back the tears. They're tears for Olivia—but I think they're also tears for me.

Chapter Forty-Two

Savannah
(23 Years Old)

Day 6,864

It was just a plea of a woman to a man she loved...from another time. But it was enough for me.

"Jake."

"Savannah."

He stands and makes his way to the front of his desk.

But I stop right inside his office door. I don't go

any farther. "I have to talk to you," I say, nervously biting my bottom lip.

"Oh." He stops short of me and falls back against the desk, crossing his legs out in front of him. "Okay."

Worry infiltrates the little lines in his forehead. And in his eyes, strangely, I can already see a sense of dread. But he can't know what I'm about to say.

It takes me a minute to gather up my courage. I breathe in. I breathe out. I can hear my heart pounding so loudly; it's as if it's echoing off my eardrums.

"Salem," he says.

I freeze and look into his eyes.

His face is expressionless. The worry, the dread— it's gone now.

My lips part—to maybe ask a question, I'm not sure. But either way, nothing comes out. And he only shrugs his strong shoulders and faintly smiles.

"It's him, right?" he asks.

I don't know how he knows. I'm at a loss for words, but I force myself to say something, anything.

"Jake, I didn't know. I swear I didn't know."

He looks down at his black, polished shoes. Then he folds his arms over his chest.

"I know you didn't." He meets my gaze. "But I did. And maybe it was wrong of me to withhold that information."

I cautiously suck in a breath.

"But do you blame me?" he asks, smiling softly.

To speak feels as if it would be the hardest thing in this world to do, so I just shake my head, instead.

His chest rises and falls. And then all of a sudden, there's a question on his face.

"Is he marri...?"

"I don't know," I say, cutting him off. "I'm crazy. I

don't even know if he's married." I try to smile, but I don't think it ever reaches my face.

He bows his head but keeps his calm demeanor.

"But it's a risk worth taking," he says.

I look at him. I look into his beautiful dark eyes. They're so loving, so understanding, so patient. I tell myself I will regret this, but deep inside my bones, I don't think I believe it.

I nod. "It is...a risk worth taking."

And then, his soft smile turns sad. And I don't know if it's sad for him or sad for me or sad for the both of us.

"I'm sorry," I say, trying not to cry. I wish I could take this all from him. There's a part of me that wishes I had never met him—then I could spare him from this. But then there's the selfish part of me that also can't imagine never knowing him.

"Don't be. I think I knew it all along."

"But how?" I ask.

"You forget. I have one, too. ...And I also took the risk, once upon a time."

I nod, as it all starts to make a little more sense now.

"But you're not..." I stop because I'm not altogether sure how to finish that sentence.

His shoulder slightly lifts and then sinks. "It doesn't always work out," he says. "But..." He looks down at the floor briefly before finding my eyes again. "But every once in a while, the odds have got to be in your favor, right?"

I'm motionless, speechless, as my heart breaks for him and for everything we could have been.

"It was nice getting to know you, Savannah Catesby."

Laura Miller

I smile because, at the very least, he deserves that simple gesture.
Even as my heart breaks, I smile.

Chapter Forty-Three

Savannah
(23 Years Old)

Day 6,865

I pull up to a building with *Ebenezer Lumber* stretched across its roof in big, orange letters. And I stop the car.

I'm in Iowa.

And this is crazy, I know. But I have to do it.

I tuck the keys into my purse and push open the driver's side door. There are a million thoughts running through my mind, but mostly, they all either have to do with anticipation or fear. I try to block them out as I make my way across the parking lot.

The two glass doors automatically part when I

reach the building. And instantly, my nose is filled with the scent of newly cut lumber and fresh paint. I breathe it in and breathe out a smile. It reminds me of Eben.

My hands start to shake. I grab the straps of my purse to try and hide their trembling.

"Uh, hi," I say to the first person I see wearing a navy, collared shirt.

A young girl, maybe in her late teens, stops in front of me.

"Is Salem Ebenezer working today?"

"Uh, yeah," the girl says, "I think he's back in his office."

I feel my heart start to race.

"Okay," I whisper.

"Do you want me to get him for you?"

"Um, no," I quickly say. "Could you just point me in the direction of his office."

"Sure." She gives me a friendly smile. "It's just back in the left corner, next to customer service."

"Okay. Thank you."

The girl goes back to stacking small boxes onto a shelf. I, on the other hand, stare apprehensively at the back of the building. I think I'm equal parts terrified and giddy. A thought runs through my head that I should just turn around and run back to my car. But then just as quickly, another thought tells me to run to his office—to run to him—and wrap my arms around him and hold him, hold him until he tells me to let go.

I decide on something in between those two thoughts, and I steadily walk toward the back of the building, in the direction the girl pointed me.

The customer service table appears way too soon, and I look to the left and find an open door to an office.

I stop. There's no one at customer service. I'm more than thankful. I don't think I could have managed to get a decent-sounding word out to someone else.

I close my eyes briefly and then take a deep breath. Then cautiously, I walk to the open door and look up.

I see Eben. But then I see Anna.

They don't see me.

I don't even think. I just turn and start walking.

I walk until I'm through the store and across the parking lot and into my car.

And it's not until then that the tears start burning the backs of my eyelids.

Every hope I had was in today—in that moment. But then, I saw... Then, I saw *her*. And in that instant, I felt the weight of this crazy idea.

Tears start falling down my cheeks. I try to wipe them with the back of my hand, but no sooner do I get them wiped away, new ones come.

He loves her.

He...loves...her.

He doesn't love me.

The tears have turned into sobs. I rest my head on the steering wheel and press my hand to my heart. The pain in my chest feels as if it's crushing my bones.

This is it. This is the end of our story.

I cry. I cry for me. I cry for us. I cry because it's the only thing I can think to do.

And I don't know how long the tears fall, but eventually, I lift my head. And I take a breath, and I wipe my puffy eyes. And I stare out the blurry windshield. And I think: *Where do I go from here?*

And then, through a new stream of tears, and against everything I believe, I hear a little voice rise up. It whispers its name: *Surrender.* And then it says: *You need to let it be. You need to let this be...and not because you want to or because it's the right thing to do, but because this is life. And sometimes, you can't write life in your own words—no matter how beautiful the words.*

Sometimes, it just is.

Chapter Forty-Four

Savannah
(24 Years Old)

Day 7,263

"**A**re you sure you want to run this?"

Jan is holding up the page with my weekly editorial piece on it.

I smile.

"Yeah. It's Valentine's Day. It fits. So, yeah, run it."

Jan just nods.

"But they'll know," she says, giving me a motherly-like smile.

"They already know."

"Okay." She nods again, right before she disappears into the other room.

Meanwhile, I swivel around in my desk chair, until I'm facing my computer screen. And I stare at the little folder on the desktop that reads tomorrow's date.

It's been about a year since the last time I set eyes on Salem. And I've seen Jake around, but we're back to small talk. I don't know if the damage I caused is irreversible, but for now, we're just keeping a safe distance.

I stare at that little folder on my computer's screen, until eventually, I take a deep breath, and I click on it. And I read the careful words I've written—the words everyone in this town will be talking about soon enough:

An Open Letter to the Girl Who Has His Heart

We share the same heart—you and I.

The only difference is:
Where it once beat for me,
Now, it only beats for you.

So, take this letter as you will.
It was never meant to slight.
It's just a little reminder,
That once that heart was mine.

That once those old photos
Were real moments,
That once that old tee shirt
Was brand new.

That once that old story

A Bird on a Windowsill

Hadn't happened yet.
All this,
Before you.

And you very well might have his last kiss.
But remember, I had his first.
And his heart—
I had that first, too.

But in the end, his past is all I have,
But please don't think I love him less.
For that boy who stole my heart,
Is now the man who holds my past.

And for that, I'll always hold a piece of him,
But remember, you'll have the whole.

For there are always moments we cannot take back,
There are regrets we can't rewind,
But there's this thing that keeps me moving;
I fondly call it time.

And in time, my mind will find peace,
Though, I'm not so certain of my soul.

For in those quiet hours,
I often hear its call.

It murmurs, wordlessly,
The lyrics I know so well:
You love him.
You love him still.

And so it is,
My song,
Set on repeat,

My soul,
Ever looking back.

But as for you,
The girl who has what I cannot,
I ask one favor,
Take care of his heart.

Take care of our *heart.*

Chapter Forty-Five

Savannah
(24 Years Old)

"**S**avannah, I'm going to get some lunch. You want anything?" Jan asks.

I look up at the clock on the wall. It's exactly noon. For a split-second, I wonder where the morning's gone.

"Uh, no," I say to Jan. "Thank you."

"Okay. Be back soon."

I watch as she pulls her coat off the rack and sticks her arms through its holes. And the next thing I hear is that little bell above the door.

I hit *save* on my computer and begin typing. But after a few moments, I hear the bell clanging in the front of the office again, and I stop.

"Savannah."

Before I can do anything else, Jake is standing in my doorway.

"Hey," he says.

I clear my throat and try to swallow.

"Hey." I push my chair back from my desk. I'd stand, but I'm too thrown off to figure out if that's what I should do.

"Do you have a minute?" he asks.

I stare into his eyes. I think I'm half hoping they'll tell me why he's here.

"Uh, yeah. Do you want to sit down?" I point to the old, blue recliner.

"Sure," he says, eyeing the chair.

He sits down, and I turn my own chair so that I'm facing him. And for just a fraction of a moment, I think of Salem. It's strange seeing Jake in the same chair that Salem always inhabited.

"I saw this week's paper," he says.

I breathe in deeply, but I don't say anything.

"I take it things didn't work out...with him?"

I softly clear my throat, hoping it will buy me some time. His question has such an honest quality to it. I can't even be mad at the fact that he just went for it.

"No," I say. "It didn't work out."

He gives me a sad, candid look, and instantly, I feel bad for not only him, but also for myself. I lost Salem at the same time I lost Jake.

"But it's okay. I had to try, right?"

He nods once. "Yeah," he agrees.

The room grows silent—that kind of silence that screams. I drop my eyes to the carpet, secretly praying for an end to the high-pitched cries, engulfing us.

"That's how it goes sometimes." His words make me look up. "Sometimes, a love lasts for a lifetime. Sometimes, it's just a few years or a few months...or a few days, even. But love is love," he says, smiling, promisingly. "It's all the same. It feels like home when it finds us, but it hurts like hell when it leaves us."

I feel my eyes starting to water, and my stare goes straight to that brown carpet again. It's uncontrollable. I don't know where the tears come from, and I don't know how to get them to go away.

"But Savannah."

Instinctively, I look up at him, and I pray that he doesn't notice my eyes.

"You're gonna make it," he says.

I smile. I don't know how I do it, but I do. I smile, and my shoulders relax. And my heart feels a little lighter, somehow.

His words are so simple. I've told myself that same thing almost a million times now. But I guess I just needed to hear someone else say it.

"He won't," he says, regaining my attention. "He won't. ...But you will."

I take a second to let his words sink in, and then I feel my brows gradually knitting together.

"Savannah." He says my name and then lowers his gaze to the floor. "A man can't be loved by you and survive it."

A small grin resurfaces on his chiseled face, while my heart breaks. It sounds too poetic to ever be true. But it's too beautiful not to take it and hold onto it for a little while.

"And I only knew you for a small piece of your life. Imagine if I would have known you from the start."

I try my best to hide my tears. "Thank you," I

whisper.

He stands and gives me a small nod before making his way to the door.

"I'm here if you need anything."

I try to smile. "Okay."

He holds a fixed stare in my eyes only for a few heartbeats. Then, he turns and leaves.

I wait for that little bell above the door, and on its cue, I let the tears fall.

I feel broken, like a tall oak after a summer storm. My trunk is splintered and torn.

How sad is it that we only have one life to live—that we can't simultaneously live two lives at once and be happy?

I wipe my tears with the back of my hand, mindfully telling myself to take deep breaths.

And then, just when I think I've pulled myself together again, I hear that little bell.

I hide my face behind my computer screen and try to look busy. I'm waiting for Jan to walk past my office. I'm waiting for the smell of Caleb's Diner to fill the room. But I never see Jan.

I wipe my eyes again and run my fingers through my hair, trying my best to appear presentable. Then I push back my chair, stand and make my way to the front.

But no sooner do I get to my office door than I stop. And every part of my body turns to ice.

Chapter Forty-Six

Savannah
(24 Years Old)

Day 7,267

I force myself to take a breath.

"Salem."

My hand lifts to tuck a piece of my hair behind my ear. I don't even realize I'm doing it, until it's done.

"Can we walk?" he asks.

I'm speechless for a good few seconds.

"Okay," I finally agree.

I grab my coat off the rack. And then I follow him out of the little newspaper office, locking the door behind me.

And we walk—in silence. We walk until we reach that little stream behind the building, and we stop.

"I read your letter." He says the words evenly, without any expression whatsoever in his voice.

I laugh, and the action surprises me. "I have a wider circulation than I thought."

He looks my way, and he smiles, faintly. But I can tell he doesn't know what to say.

"I didn't know if you'd see it," I say. "It was just something I needed to say. I'm sorry if it..."

His eyes find mine, and I lose my words. His stare is warm and comfortable, even though I feel as if it should feel far away.

"I didn't mean anything by it." I nervously bite my bottom lip. "I mean, I meant it, but I didn't want to upset anyone."

"Savannah."

I stop when I hear his calm, familiar voice. And I take a quick breath.

"It didn't matter who you chose."

I force the breath out slowly.

"It didn't matter who you chose, Vannah. The result was always going to be the same."

My heart stings in my chest. And I fight the tears; I fight the tears that seem to come from some bottomless well deep inside my soul.

"I just wanted you to know that," he breathes out.

I nod and lower my head, but I can't stop thinking about how much I love him. I want him more than I want anything in this whole world. And I can't have him.

He clears his throat, forcing my attention back to him. The tears are blurring my vision, but nevertheless, I watch as he pulls out a piece of paper from his coat pocket.

It's folded and then folded again.

"Here," he says, "it's a letter to the editor."

I look into his light eyes and then slowly reach for the page. And when I get it open, my own eyes go to reading his handwritten words:

An Open Letter to the Girl Who Still Has My Heart

We share the same heart—you and I.

Where mine beats,
I feel yours, too.

It beats for every story,
Every memory,
Every moment,
We call ours.

And in it,
We store our weakness,
Our armor,
Our scars.

But most of all,
Our secret—

That we'd never really move on.

And of course, you have my past,
But that's never all you had.

For when you stole my heart,
You also took my last:

My last dream,

My last love,
My last kiss,
My last breath.

It's only fitting; you had them first.

So, to the beautiful bird who still has my heart,
It's yours to keep.

For as much as it's mine, it's yours.

I finish reading.

"See, the funny thing is," he says, in a soft, rasping voice, "when I think of you...or I see you, every girl fades from my mind...every girl, but you."

My eyes slowly find his.

"Vannah, all I know how to do is love you."

I try to swallow down the tears as I stare into his eyes.

"I might be awful at telling you the right way, but I *know* how to love you." He stops, and a soft smile fights its way to his face. "And it didn't matter who you chose," he says, shaking his head. "Because I chose you. I choose you, Vannah." He shrugs and pierces my stare. "I choose you."

I'm wordless. An endless stream of tears is sliding down my cheeks. My breaths are short.

"I... I don't understand," I say.

"Vannah, I had already chosen you, a long time ago."

I feel my chest lifting and falling, but it's hard to get a breath.

"Vannah, I never asked her to marry me."

My brow furrows.

"But I saw her with you in Iowa."

"In Iowa?" He cocks his head and gives me a questioning look.

I nod. "I went to the lumberyard almost a year ago to tell you...basically what I wrote in the letter. I wanted to change our story."

He stops.

"Like Olivia wanted Lester to?" he asks.

"You saw the photo?"

He nods. And then he smiles.

"She was only there a minute, dropping off the rest of my things." He takes a step closer to me. "You have impeccable timing, Miss Catesby."

My teeth press into my bottom lip as my mouth curves up.

"She wasn't you, Vannah."

I stop and find his eyes.

"So," he whispers, his face so close to mine that I can almost feel the word tumbling from his lips, "do you still think we've got a chance?"

I bow my head and then slowly nod. And in the next second, his arms are around me, squeezing me into his chest.

I'm just wrapping my mind around this moment, around him being here, around his letter, around the fact that he's holding me in his arms.

"It took seeing your letter in the paper," he whispers softly in my ear. "I guess I just needed to breathe for myself first."

I smile through my tears.

"But it was nice falling in love with you...again and again and again," he whispers.

Then he pulls away and looks into my eyes. In his eyes, I can still see that look—that longing, that same longing look he gave me when we were only sixteen.

The memory rushes over me like a soft summer breeze, full of the smell of life and risk and chance.

He draws closer to me, and I can feel his every breath hit my lips. I close my eyes, and he weaves his hand into my hair.

"I've missed you so much," he whispers. "I never stopped missing you."

And just then, I don't care how many years we've lost; I don't care how many mistakes we've made; I don't care how long it took us to get here. We're here. ...We're here, and that's all that matters.

And in the next heartbeat, his lips touch mine. And with my heart wide open, I spread my wings—and fly.

Chapter Forty-Seven
Savannah
(24 Years Old)

Day 7,277

"Close your eyes."

"They're closed," I say.

"Okay, two more steps."

I shuffle my feet over the leaf-covered ground.

"Okay, you ready?" he asks.

"Yes."

"Open them."

I open my eyes and see a structure—a tall, beautiful, red-brick building—lit up in the night. It's cylinder in shape, two stories, with a dome top. And there's a little walkway with a railing that wraps around the dome. And there are windows perfectly placed all around the first floor and around the dome as well. It's like something I've never seen before.

"I found our star tower," he whispers near my ear.

My mouth opens, but nothing comes out. I just keep staring at that beautiful little building in the middle of all the trees.

"Eben," I exclaim, just trying to take it all in.

"Come on," he says. "You want to see it, right?"

I look at him for a few seconds, asking him a million silent questions, all at once. But he just stares back at me with a crooked smile glued to his face.

"Yes," I finally say. "Yes, I want to see it."

We walk up the few brick stairs to a wooden door, painted emerald. And he sticks a key into the lock and turns the knob. Then he pushes open the big door, and we both step inside.

Immediately, I notice the freestanding staircase that starts at the floor and spirals all the way up to the ceiling, two stories up.

My hand covers my mouth as my gaze roams around the room and stops on a photo of a beach at sunrise. There are seagulls in the sand. The sky is orange; the ocean is white. I can almost smell the salty air. And there are more—more photos of the ocean. They're all framed and hung on the wall. It's all so beautiful. But I stop when my eyes catch on a spot in the far corner of the room.

"Are those mine?"

He nods. "Yep. Those two boxes were my motivation. It's your stuff, for when you came back."

I find his eyes, and my heart breaks for the eighteen-year-old boy who stored his hope in two cardboard boxes all these years, waiting for his bird to come home. But he only smiles, takes my hand and leads me up the wooden staircase.

Up and around we spiral, until we reach the second floor. And right away, I notice the big telescope in the middle of the room, pointing to the center of the dome.

"I just can't believe you did all of this," I say.

He only shrugs.

I walk toward the telescope, but I stop when I see the walls. They're covered in our memories. The Polaroids. Each frame floats against the red brick. He must have taken the photos from my house when I wasn't looking.

I pause at each photo. Each one tells a different story. The first is of an old quote about being forgotten etched into a wooden park bench. But I look deeper, and I feel what it's like to always be remembered.

I run my fingers gently over the glass of the next photo. It's of a sea of green fields where our names live forever. I can almost hear our voices bouncing off those tall, dirt levees.

I move to the third photo. It's of an attractive man with strong features and almond skin, who's wearing a smile that says *I love you.*

I wish I had seen that back then.

Two bricks down, there's another frame, and inside of it, another photo. This photo is nothing but black, yet I can still see that old sawdust pile and those weathered wooden boards of his parents' dock. And I see the moonlight reflecting off the creek water at Hogan's slab, and I can feel our hearts beating.

And there are others. Photos of me. Photos of him. Photos of all the places we've spent time together. All the Polaroids we ever took together—they're all here.

I move my fingers over each one, barely grazing the glass. And with each one, I briefly close my eyes— remembering the strength of the deep blues and the dark grays and the smell of rain and October and sweet tea. And I remember what it's like to live in each one— to feel like the ocean at dusk in the summer, peacefully pushing its way to the shore, only to relent and then press on again—never thinking, ever moving.

And then, when I've made my way all around the room, I stop. And I look at him.

"Those are for me," he says, smiling. "But this is for you." He rests his hand on the wall.

I give him a questioning look, right before he flips a little switch. And instantly, the room grows dark.

We wait there, perfectly still, until gradually, tiny, white stars start springing forth from the walls.

I gasp. "Eben."

"Alongside the stars, right?" he asks.

I glance at him and then back at the hundreds of tiny white lights all over the walls.

"It's beautiful," I say, spinning slowly in a circle, my eyes never leaving the stars.

And then I stop and find him.

"I can't believe you did this."

"I didn't. I found it."

I search the shades of brown in his eyes—those I can see in the little light that surrounds us.

"Are we on Sheppard's Hill?"

He takes a breath and then nods. "We are."

Then he walks toward me and wraps his arms around me.

"Thank you," I whisper near his ear.

He squeezes me tighter.

"It's nothing. A very wise man once told me: 'you find a girl that gives you a piece of her treasure, you hold onto that treasure. And better yet, you hold onto that girl.' And I guess that's what I did."

I let my head rest against his chest. My heart is beating wildly. I can't stop smiling.

"Savannah Catesby," he whispers, "I've definitely touched things with half of my heart before, but you were never one of them."

I feel his lips touch my forehead.

"I'm in love with you, Savannah. ...I always have been."

I press my cheek to his chest and breathe him in. "Salem Ebenezer...I'm so in love with you." I pull away from his embrace and find his gaze. "And I plan on spending the rest of this life falling *in love* with you more and more every day."

He smiles, and I swear my heart does, too. And then he leans away and reaches for another switch. And just like that, a piece of the dome above us starts to peel back.

I'm wonderstruck, just watching that night sky come alive above us.

"Eben..."

He shakes his head slowly back and forth, instantly halting my thought.

"It was here all along. You built it in your mind. I just organized the bricks and the boards. That's all."

I look into his eyes, praying he can see how much I love him. And after a moment, he gently takes my hand and leads me up the few little stairs to the raised platform.

"Go ahead." He eyes the small mouth of the telescope. "It's another world."

I move my eye over it, and just like that, I'm floating. I'm floating in a sea of thousands of painted stars in a universe far above ours.

"It's like I'm there," I say.

Eben flips another switch, and the roof starts retracting in pieces. I look up and just watch in awe as the night fills the little room.

And after a minute, when the sky is all that's above us, I notice an open space on the platform, so I go to it and lie back against the wood.

He smiles and then finds a spot next to me.

When he's settled, I take his hand. His touch feels like a thousand memories hitting my fingertips all at once.

"Why did you do this? All of this?"

He shrugs. "Because I made a promise. I said I would always look up at the sky with you. And even if I couldn't have you—like this, by my side—at least I'd still have you. I built you into the walls of this place."

I let his words—as if they're spoken from his very soul—sink in. They fill my heart and then spill over.

"Until we're thirty?" I ask.

He laughs softly. "Until we're one hundred and thirty."

I smile. And then, the world around us grows still.

"Eben."

He looks my way.

"If I had never come back, would we be here right now?"

He keeps his gaze in mine for the length of time it takes a bird to spread its wings, and then his focus travels to the black sky.

"I don't know. I'd like to think that it was meant to be—that someday, we'd eventually cross paths again."

"But would it have been too late?" I ask.

He breathes in deeply and then breathes out a sigh. "Maybe."

The weight of his word is almost too heavy to bear.

"But still, nothing would have changed," he says, looking into my eyes again. "I was always going to love you. No matter if you were right here next to me or all the way up there, sitting beside that man in the moon." He points to that big, round light in the sky. "I was going to love you; I had already conceded to that much. And I guess, before you came back, I was thinking the cards had already been dealt for us. I figured you had moved on and taken my heart with you. And I guess I had just hoped I'd find a way to love without it. But as it turns out, I think you can only really love with your heart."

A soft laugh plays on his lips. And the sound of his broken voice slowly begins to lift the anvil from my chest.

"If you try to love with anything else, you won't get too far; trust me. Your gut is too cautious. Your mind is too rational. But the heart," he says, "the heart is just crazy enough."

He smiles wide. And I squeeze his hand. And at the same time, I feel my own heart swell—with love, with joy, with understanding.

"You know, I used to dream about you," I say.

He brushes a strand of my hair away from my face. His touch is like suddenly remembering a favorite moment you had long forgotten. It warms every part of me.

"When I was gone, when I came back," I say. "I don't even know where they came from...or why. But you'd always be holding my hand."

His smile fades a little, as if he's in thought.

"I could feel every real sensation of your thumb rubbing the back of my hand. And when I'd wake up, I'd remember the dream—everything about it, including the way you looked at me. It's as if you looked at me to say: *Always*."

"Always," he repeats, in a soft whisper.

"Mm hmm. And I rested in the fact that no one could touch that—that no one could break it or bend it into something different. It made me feel as if no matter what—no matter where we were or who we were with or what place in time we existed—I would be yours...and you would be mine."

He squeezes my hand.

"I held onto that, I think," I say. "Those dreams were so real. I held onto them."

His head bobs slowly up and down.

"That's what love does," he says, looking into my eyes. "It takes over every part of us—even our dreams—if only just to remind us where our heart is, where it will always be."

He brings my hand to his lips and softly kisses my fingertips. Then he presses our intertwined hands to his heart and returns his gaze to the world above us.

But I keep my eyes on him, as a tear trickles down my cheek.

He was always my moon,

my stars,

my world.

Epilogue One

Savannah

Day 25,551

My name is Savannah Catesby. And this is my love story.

It's not pretty. And it's definitely not poetry. But as it turns out, it does have a happy ending.

I married Salem Ebenezer on a warm day in September. The maples were just beginning to turn. The smell of dried leaves and sycamore filled the air. And I looked into his beautiful, sandy eyes, and I said: "I do." And he said: "Always."

That was nearly fifty years ago to date.

A lot of life is lived in fifty years. And then again,

fifty years feels like a blink of an eye.

Some days, I just stare into our Polaroids on the wall in our star tower, and I swear that they were taken just yesterday. I swear, just yesterday, Eben and I were under those stairs in junior high, talking and dreaming. And just last night, I swear, our backs were pressed against that concrete at Hogan's slab. I can even feel the heat from the rock seeping into my bare skin. But mostly, I just feel the way his thumb caressed the back of my sun-tanned hand.

Those were our Polaroid years. Those were the years we didn't think much beyond the way the afternoon sun felt on our faces or how the cool creek water stung every inch of our skin. And that's precisely why I love them.

But then those Polaroid years melted into something even more beautiful, I think. They melted into a life we called *ours*.

Eben and I had three children: two boys, one girl. One of the boys is now running Ebenezer Lumber. All of our children are married and happy, and now they have children of their own—our grandchildren.

And then again, some things never change. Eben never sold his old truck. In fact, it still runs today. And every time I look at it, I feel that old woven fabric and vinyl sticking to my skin and the wind from the scoop in my hair. And it's funny, but I can still feel the way my body swayed at every hill and turn, as we wore out a path from his house to mine.

And to this day, there's a key that hangs around Eben's neck. I made a copy and gave his back to him the day we wed. It reminds us of being young. And it reminds us of his grandpa, my Uncle Lester and Olivia. But most of all, it reminds us that sometimes we need to stop and remember where our hearts are—where they've always been, where they'll always be.

And yet, when the night is at rest and the darkness is silent, I still just can't help but think sometimes how, fifty years ago, we almost missed out on love.

But of course, love would never allow that. See, it never leaves us. *We* just have to *choose* it.

And on that cool, February day, at the place where we first began, we took back our story—we chose love.

Because I think, deep down, we both decided, somewhere along the line, to throw out all the truths we ever learned about life, except one:

Sometimes the hearts we steal are not the hearts we were ever meant to keep.

But then, sometimes...they are.

Epilogue Two

Salem

Day 28,105

People say birds are a bad omen.
They're wrong.

My name is Salem Ebenezer. But as you know,
you can call me *Eben*.

I fell in love with Savannah Elise Catesby a long
time ago. I can't exactly tell you if it was on Day One or
Day 4,592. But I can tell you that on that very first day I

saw her at that little creek that crawled right through the center of our little hometown, she stole my heart.

And I've never once asked for it back.

But then again, the mind gets foggy over time. And the things you thought you'd never lose sight of, somehow, you do. Because one day, I forgot she had my heart, and I almost lost her for it.

See, on that day I was asking her to choose, I had forgotten something. I had forgotten that I had already made my choice long before she ever had a chance to say a word. And that's all that really mattered. Because no matter what she said or didn't say, I loved her. I loved Savannah Catesby. That was my answer. That was the story I would forever tell; that was the dream I would forever live in. I would love her. I would love her with every breath I took—until my last.

So, yes, while she didn't choose me that day, I sure as hell chose her.

And I still chose her every day after that.

I chose her every morning before the sun came up and the air was cool and I found her under the covers and I pressed my skin to hers.

I chose her every afternoon in those moments where my mind would drift back to the days when her hair was short and our adventures were long.

I chose her every evening when the sun was tiptoeing on that orange horizon and she was in my arms, telling me about her day.

And every night, when we were climbing the stairs in our little home, next to our little star tower on Sheppard's Hill, I chose her.

And I can't tell you how my life would have turned out had she not come home. I only know that my heart would have always been with her.

I'm eighty-two today. I'm standing with a cane in a field next to a little, stone church. I'm not alone. Although some might say I am, I'm not.

Vannah's here. She's in my heart.

A lot of people came up to me yesterday and gave me their sympathies and reminded me that we had fifty-seven good years together. I always corrected them and said: *We had seventy-seven. We had seventy-seven good years together.*

Seventy-seven years. The number makes it seem as though it was enough. But it wasn't.

"Vannah..." My voice catches, and I start again. "Vannah, it hasn't even been a day, and I've already forgotten how I like my toast. I didn't even realize, until this morning, that you always made it for me. And there are other things, too. I've forgotten if I take two sugars or one; you always knew. I've even forgotten how I filled my days because for the last day, I've only been doing what you always enjoyed doing: I've fed your hummingbirds; I've watched the cooking channel; and I've organized your gardening magazines.

But there are some things I haven't forgotten. I haven't forgotten which chair is yours; it's pushed under the table. I stared at it for a long time this morning, pretending you were just at your sister's for breakfast. And I haven't forgotten what side of the porch swing was your favorite—the right. You said it was because you could see the kids coming down the road first and you could jump up and get supper on the table. But I knew better. You liked the right side because from that side, you could see my old truck. I would catch you smiling at it every once in a while. I know you missed being young in that old vinyl just as much as I do."

I grow quiet as a warm breeze pushes past me. Then carefully, I lean against my cane and gently set a photo down onto the ground next to the stone that reads her name. It's the Polaroid of those green fields in the river bottoms.

"They're still there, *V*. I want you to remember that our names are still there, bouncing off those levees."

I take a handkerchief from my shirt pocket and wipe my eyes.

"I want you to remember that they'll always be there—yours and mine, together."

I pause and look at her name etched in that stone: *Savannah (Vannah) Elise Ebenezer.*

The second death.

I use the handkerchief to wipe my eyes some more. They leak the more my heart longs for her gentle touch—just one more time.

"There was a second," I say to her. "We couldn't help that. But there won't be a third, my bird."

And from somewhere deep inside my soul, a sob escapes me.

"I miss you, Vannah."

I stare into that photo against the turned-up dirt, and I think about the only girl who ever had my heart. And I don't know how much time the good Lord has me down here still, but I do know this for sure: I was made to love a little girl with short blond hair and green eyes, who liked stars and made up stories about magic keys. I was put here to love her. And until my last breath, that's what I'll keep doing. And I'll keep loving her right into the next life, too. Because it doesn't matter the day or the hour or the life—I choose her. I'll always choose her because bottom line, I never really had a choice. She was just a bird on a windowsill. But she was always *my bird.*

The End

The future for me is already a thing of the past. You were my first love and you will be my last.
~Bob Dylan

ACKNOWLEDGMENTS

There are so many people who have touched my writing career and this book, in particular, that I can't possibly fit all my gratitude for them into one book, much less one page. But here is my best attempt at thanking a few of you.

As always, I thank God, my greatest inspiration, for giving me the opportunity to write each and every day.

And thank you to my amazing editors and sources for all your time and contributions. Thank you especially to Donna, Calvin, Kathy, April, Sharon, Jon, Jesse and Mike. Thank you from the bottom of my heart. None of my stories would be what they are today without you!

And thank you to my newspaper friends and former editors, including Steve, John, Tom, Bruce and Andy. Thank you for teaching me how to tell a story. Today, the stories might be different, but my mind is never far away from that black ink. [The] *wise shall be the bearers of light. ~Walter Williams*

And thank YOU, for reading. I know there are so many stories out there. Thank you for taking a chance on my small-town characters. Thank you for taking the ride with them—for pulling for them, for cheering them on. And as always, thank you for cheering me on!

And a special thank you also goes to the amazing bloggers all over the world for their enthusiasm and loyal support and love of fairy tales. Know that we, as writers, are ever grateful for your commitment to literature.

I would also like to thank my family, including Jack, Aurora and Levi, who continues to be my biggest fans and greatest supporters. And thank you also to my friends and mentors, who are ever inspiring me.

And lastly but definitely not least, I would like to thank my husband, Neville. Thank you for your constant encouragement from the very beginning of this grand adventure. Honey, you steal my heart every day. And I'll never ask for it back. I love you!

Photo by Neville Miller

LAURA MILLER is the national best-selling author of the novels: *Butterfly Weeds, My Butterfly, For All You Have Left, By Way of Accident, When Cicadas Cry, A Bird on a Windowsill* and *The Life We Almost Had*. She grew up in Missouri, graduated from the University of Missouri-Columbia and worked as a newspaper reporter prior to writing fiction. Laura currently lives in the Midwest with her husband. Visit her and learn more about her books at LauraMillerBooks.com.

ALSO BY LAURA MILLER

Butterfly Weeds
My Butterfly
For All You Have Left
By Way of Accident
When Cicadas Cry
The Life We Almost Had

"One of the most beautiful love stories I have ever read."
~Jelena's Book Blog on *Butterfly Weeds*

★★★★★ **"THIS IS PURE ROMANCE AT ITS BEST."**
~Kathy Reads Fiction on *My Butterfly*

★★★★★ **"UNPUTDOWNABLE!"**
~Southern Belle Book Blog on *For All You Have Left*

"Newcomers will have their faith in good literature restored."
~Books to Breathe on *By Way of Accident*

"One of the most beautiful stories and cherished romances."
~Kathy Reads Fiction on *When Cicadas Cry*

"ONE OF MY FAVORITE LOVE STORIES EVER."
~A Novel Review on *For All You Have Left*

★★★★★ **#MUSTREAD #BEAUTIFUL #CAPTIVATING**
~Nancy's Romance Reads on *By Way of Accident*

"THE BOOK THAT FEEDS MY WANT OF THE PERFECT ROMANCE."
~The Bookie Rookie on *The Life We Almost Had*